"A Good Man Is Hard to Find"

VOLUMES IN THE SERIES

CHARLOTTE PERKINS GILMAN, "The Yellow Wallpaper"
Edited by Thomas L. Erskine and Connie L. Richards, Salisbury State University

FLANNERY O'CONNOR, "A Good Man Is Hard to Find"
Edited by Frederick Asals, University of Toronto

KATHERINE ANNE PORTER, "Flowering Judas"
Edited by Virginia Spencer Carr, Georgia State University

LESLIE MARMON SILKO, "Yellow Woman"
Edited by Melody Graulich, University of New Hampshire

ALICE WALKER, "Everyday Use"
Edited by Barbara Christian, University of California, Berkeley

HISAYE YAMAMOTO, "Seventeen Syllables"
Edited by King-Kok Cheung, University of California, Los Angeles

"A Good Man Is Hard to Find"

FLANNERY O'CONNOR

Edited and with an introduction by
FREDERICK ASALS

Rutgers University Press
New Brunswick, New Jersey

Library of Congress Cataloging-in-Publication Data

O'Connor, Flannery.
A good man is hard to find / Flannery O'Connor ; edited and with an introduction by Frederick Asals.
p. cm. — (Women writers : text and contexts)
Includes bibliographical references.
ISBN 0-8135-1976-4 (cloth) — ISBN 0-8135-1977-2 (paper)
1. O'Connor, Flannery. Good man is hard to find. 2. Women and literature—United States—History—20th century. I. Asals, Frederick. II. Title. III. Series: Women writers (New Brunswick, N.J.)
PS3565.C57G6 1993
813'.54—dc20 92-39505
CIP

British Cataloging-in-Publication information available.

Manufactured in the United States of America

Contents

Introduction

FREDERICK ASALS

Introduction

I

"A Good Man Is Hard to Find" is probably now, as during her lifetime, the single story by which Flannery O'Connor is best known. She herself may have had something to do with this: when she was asked to give a reading or a talk to students, "A Good Man" was the story she usually proposed. As she wrote to John Hawkes, she preferred a reading with commentary to a lecture because "It's better to try to make one story live for them than to tell them a lot of junk they'll forget in five minutes and that I have no confidence in anyhow."[1] It was not, she claimed, her favorite among her stories (that honor she accorded "The Artificial Nigger"); she chose "A Good Man" for public readings (or so a friend told me) because it was the only one she could get through and not "bust out laughing."

Whatever force these readings had in establishing the story, she had already singled it out by making it the title piece of her first collection, published in 1955 (*A Good Man Is Hard to Find and Other Stories*). That alone might not have sufficed to give it preeminence (when the collection was published in England it bore, without authorial permission, the title *The Artificial Nigger*). In 1960, however, her friends Allen Tate and Caroline Gordon selected it for inclusion in the second edition of their enormously influential anthology, *The House of Fiction*, and thus began the history of "A Good Man" as a favorite of anthologizers. Its only rival among her work at the time was, once more, "The Artificial Nigger," which had been anthologized earlier, but in less powerful places. By 1966, W. S. Marks III could speak casually of "A Good Man" as "one of the more frequently anthologized of her pieces." More recently, other stories, including those from her second collection, *Everything That Rises Must Converge,* have displaced it as an inevitable choice of anthologists, but it was established for long enough to remain the single tale most immediately associated with Flannery O'Connor.

That eminence is not entirely arbitrary or accidental. Its quality aside, the story probably makes available more rapidly and obviously than anything else she ever wrote the unsettling mix of comedy, violence, and religious concern that characterizes her fiction. Other stories may, arguably, be funnier, subtler, more moving, more resonant, but "A Good Man" brings before the reader, with a powerful shock, the main features of O'Connor's fictive world. Perhaps its place in her career helps explain why it seems to capture within its borders some essence of her vision.

"A Good Man Is Hard to Find" was first published in Avon's *Modern Writing 1* in late September 1953.[2] It was the last of the four stories she published that year, a group which, in turn, comprised her first crop of mature stories, works that she would consider worthy of putting between hard covers. Her master's thesis for the University of Iowa's Writer's Workshop had been comprised of a half-dozen stories, but these she clearly viewed as apprentice pieces, and a section cut out of her novel-in-progress and published independently in 1949 would get heavily rewritten and retitled ("A Stroke of Good Fortune") before its later admittance to her collection. O'Connor rarely sat on completed work—her usual practice was to send a story out for responses from trusted friends, make any revisions in light of their commentary, then send it on to her agent—and her letters suggest that all the stories published in 1953 ("A Late Encounter with the Enemy," "The Life You Save May Be Your Own," and "The River" were the others) were written in 1952 or early 1953. It is unlikely any were written earlier, as 1951 was taken up almost entirely with two occupations: surviving the lupus erythematosus that had suddenly struck her down in December 1950 and preparing for publication the manuscript of her first novel, *Wise Blood*.

At first glance, *Wise Blood* (1952) seems radically different from "A Good Man Is Hard to Find." It is a severely stylized novel, populated by the grotesque denizens of a nightmarish urban landscape who engage in ironically rendered verbal and physical violence while approaching their absurd or dreadful ends. At its center is Hazel Motes, grandson of a fundamentalist preacher, so desperate to be rid of Jesus that he devises and preaches a backwoods version of nihilistic existentialism with a ferocious intensity usually reserved for more orthodox creeds. As Robert Fitzgerald has pointed out, existentialism was the "last word in attitudes . . . when Flannery O'Connor began to write," and it provides a thematic link between novel and story.[3] Its postures reverberate in the rolling-stone experience of "A Good Man's" Misfit: "I been most everything. Been in the arm service, both land and sea, at home and abroad, been twict married, been an undertaker, been with the railroads, plowed Mother Earth, been in a tornado, seen a man burnt alive oncet. . . . I even seen a woman flogged." Existentialist accents sound even more clearly in his metaphysical questionings of "why it is"—why some suffer and others do not, why punishment and crime never match, why the very earth itself seems both devoid of significance and a prison. If The Misfit's stance of interrogation differs from Hazel Motes's blasphemous defiance, both postures are nonetheless assumed on a similar basis—the basis of the apparent meaninglessness of human existence in a neutralized cosmos from which the divine is absent. It is little wonder that echoes of "existentialist" writers from Dostoyevsky to Camus have been detected in The Misfit's speeches.

But if The Misfit glances back toward *Wise Blood*, his

antagonist in the story, the grandmother, has no real predecessor there. She is the first of many O'Connor figures to ground the work (as *Wise Blood* never is grounded) in what Flannery O'Connor referred to as the realm of "manners," an everyday worldliness concerned with such matters as family relations, dress and appearance, etiquette, economic and social status. Complacent and self-satisfied, these characters—and they are usually women—may well pay lip service to conventional Christianity, but their eyes are fixed firmly on the imperatives of this world. Murderously polite criminals evolved out of O'Connor's imagination working on the more sensational news of the day (see the article by J. O. Tate in this volume); genteel ladies she had known since childhood. If The Misfit seems to emerge from the wildness that produced *Wise Blood,* the grandmother looks forward to the many stories that are rooted in a recognizable Southern social milieu, and their long confrontation, both comic and violent, in the second half of "A Good Man" may be what makes this seem *the* quintessential O'Connor story.

Whenever O'Connor worked on the story, it was virtually complete by late March or early April of 1953 when she sent it off to her friends Sally and Robert Fitzgerald for their response.[4] Apparently she got one, but it seems not to have survived, and on June 7 she wrote to inform them she had sold it to the *Partisan Review Reader.* Like all her fiction, the story bears the discernible traces of its time of composition, most of which were more local in time and place than The Misfit's existential musings. The advertising for Red Sammy Butts's short order house, "filling station and dance hall" includes the patriotic claim that the proprietor is a veteran (a role he plays right down to his "khaki trousers"), a reminder that the reverberations of World War II were still to be felt in the early fifties. These were the years of the Marshall Plan of aid to war-ravaged Europe, but in the xenophobic South, this policy was likely to produce the kind of conversation that takes place between Red Sammy and the grandmother.

> He and the grandmother discussed better times. The old lady said that in her opinion Europe was entirely to blame for the way things were now. She said the way Europe acted you would think we were made of money and Red Sam said it was no use talking about it, she was exactly right.

The fifties are detectable in other touches as well: in June Star's tap dance lessons and her reference to the popular show of the fledgling medium of television, "Queen for a Day"; in the slacks and head-kerchief of the children's mother; in the country and western tune popularized nationwide by Patti Page, "The Tennessee Waltz."[5] Perhaps the atmosphere of the times is nowhere more powerfully, if indirectly, expressed than in the following passage:

> "In my time," said the grandmother, folding her thin veined fingers, "children were more respectful of their native states and their parents and everything else. People did right then. Oh look at the cute little pickaninny!" she said and pointed to a Negro child standing in the door of a shack. "Wouldn't that make a picture, now?" she asked and they all turned and looked at the little Negro out of the back window. He waved.
>
> "He didn't have any britches on," June Star said.
>
> "He probably didn't have any," the grandmother explained. "Little niggers in the country don't have things like we do. If I could paint, I'd paint that picture," she said.

The grandmother's complacency, her reduction of the moral to the picturesque (poverty as aesthetic category?), and the brilliant non-sequitur of the verb "explained"—the old lady's explanation of course illuminates nothing but the imperviousness of her kind—all expose the automatic racism of the postwar South in those years immediately preceding the civil rights movement. It is frequently noted that O'Connor virtually never made the South's racial situation her central fictional subject; it is less frequently noted that virtually every story contains at least one trenchant passage like this one that epitomizes that situation. She knew what she was about: as she wrote a friend about a pending public appearance. "I am going to read 'A Good Man Is Hard to Find,' deleting the paragraph about the little nigger who doesn't have any britches on. I can write with ease what I forbear to read" (*Habit* 317).

The local appears in other ways as well. The reference to "The Tennessee Waltz" not only fixes the temporal period of the action, but connects with the entire "Tennessee motif" in the story, which is itself part of a larger, typically Southern nostalgia. It is the note on which "A Good Man" opens: "The grandmother didn't want to go to Florida. She wanted to visit some of her connections in east Tennessee." When the song plays on the nickelodeon at Red Sammy's, the grandmother "swayed her head from side to side and pretended she was dancing in her chair"; shortly thereafter, she will "pretend" so successfully that she knows a plantation with white columns, twin arbors, and an avenue of oaks where, behind a secret panel "the family silver was hidden . . . When Sherman came through," that she will fool even herself. Not only does her deception lead the family down the fatal dirt road, but a sudden "horrible thought" produces the spasmodic reaction that precipitates the accident that leaves them all at the mercy of The Misfit—a chain of causation with the inflexibility of iron links. "The horrible thought she had had before the accident was that the house she had remembered so vividly was not in Georgia but in Tennessee."

That house, as the grandmother has joked about another antebellum plantation, is truly "Gone With the Wind. . . .

Ha. Ha." The South's nostalgia for its own supposed glorious past, its glamorous lost cause is, in O'Connor's view, a form of sentimentality that is far from harmless, that can precipitate car accidents and is not divorced from a perception of poor black children as picturesque. Born in Savannah, Georgia, she had grown up there and in Milledgeville, and had spent a half-dozen of her adult years outside of the South, yet even when she was living elsewhere—in Iowa, New York, or Connecticut—it was her native region that occupied her and provided the material of her fiction. Unlike Faulkner and other southern writers of a previous generation, she was not fascinated by the Civil War, but she was fascinated by the South's own fascination (that fascination is the subject of another of the 1953 stories, "A Late Encounter With the Enemy"). The ultimate result of this sentimental backward-looking, "A Good Man" implies, is such a figure as The Misfit, a man thrust into the moral and metaphysical vacuum that results in part from self-serving nostalgia. One of the story's nicer ironies is that down this road in an imagined "Tennessee," the grandmother has indeed come face to face with one of her "connections."

II

Serious criticism of "A Good Man Is Hard to Find" may be said to begin where widespread publication of the story began, with Caroline Gordon and Allen Tate's anthology *The House of Fiction* (1960).[6] Appearing first in 1950, *The House of Fiction* was an influential product of the most important critical movement of the time, the so-called New Criticism, which argued that each work of literature should be treated as a self-contained piece, without reference to social and political background, the author's biography, or even other works by the same writer. What could and should be analyzed, according to New Critics, was how the writer had gone about realizing the particular concerns of the individual work. As the preface to the 1960 second edition states, *The House of Fiction* "is based on the assumption that fiction is an art closely allied to painting and that, as in painting, there are certain 'constants' or secrets of technique which . . . appear in the works of all the masters of the craft" (ix). The key terms—art, craft, technique—are not interchangeable, but they are closely connected; it is indicative that the book's theoretical appendix, first called "The Arts of Fiction," is in this edition called "Notes on Fictional Techniques." Here, while such matters as action, symbolism, and unity of tone are taken up, the most important place is reserved for matters of "authority" (that is, point of view: from what angle is a story told to us? on whose "authority" is it narrated?) and "panorama" and "scene" (or telling and showing: what is told us directly? what is dramatized?). Throughout *The House of Fiction* the underlying assumption is that each story may be quite adequately discussed within the terms of the various "techniques" brought to bear on its materials.

These assumptions make it especially odd, then, that the commentary on "A Good Man" takes the turn it does, eventually moving beyond such principles. For purposes of analysis, the story is paired with Truman Capote's "The Headless Hawk." Since the essential material of these two Southern writers is so similar, we are told, their "techniques are of more than ordinary interest." For some time, we do hear about technique—comparisons of style in narrative and dialogue, for instance—and them, rather abruptly, about O'Connor's particular failure: "Her lapses result, seemingly, from her reluctance, or it may be inability, to solve the first problem which confronts any writer of fiction: on whose authority . . . is this story told?" Most readers will not notice "that she is playing fast and loose with an age-old convention; in her stories the Omniscient Narrator . . . , one who, seeing all and knowing all, has immemorially been presumed to be elevated considerably above the conflict, often speaks like a Georgia 'cracker'" (384).

This is the end of that particular point. The eager student, anxious to discover the strengths and weaknesses in such an apparently accomplished story as "A Good Man," receives no further help, no examples of such "lapses," no instance of cracker-like narrative language, no illustration of the supposed "playing fast and loose" with point of view. We now know, many years later, that one of these editors, Caroline Gordon, was in fact Flannery O'Connor's mentor throughout her mature career and that her main point of criticism on the drafts O'Connor submitted to her was, repeatedly, narrative language and waverings in point of view. So we may now guess where this part of the commentary on "A Good Man" comes from—not, probably, from a reading of the finished story, but from readings of earlier versions of that and other O'Connor works that had passed under Caroline Gordon's careful scrutiny. Indeed, a few years later, Gordon would claim that the published story exhibited "perfection of phrasing."[7]

In short, we have to go outside the bounds of the textual analysis here to explain *its* silences and omissions—just as the New Criticism on which *The House of Fiction* is based says should be unnecessary. But the commentary itself soon violates these principles actively, as well as by omission. Not only do we hear about other O'Connor works—*Wise Blood,* other stories—we also are told of the "theological framework" that governs all her fiction, a framework which is "never explicit" but "never absent." While rightly drawing attention to The Misfit's preoccupation with theological concerns, Gordon and Tate at this point leap from character to author, a shift neither explained nor justified, one which is clearly grounded in a far more extensive familiarity with O'Connor's fiction than can be gained from this single story.

These two matters raised by Gordon and Tate—the

"craft" of the story, and especially its use of point of view; and the importance of its theology—will surface again in the criticism which follows.[8] W. S. Marks III, for instance, in his "Advertisements for Grace" (1966), takes the theological perspective for granted and, while touching on a number of connections between O'Connor and other writers—from Nathaniel Hawthorne to James Baldwin—develops one of Gordon and Tate's hints ("The grandmother . . . represents the Old South") and reads the story essentially as an allegory ("Grandma Worldliwise," Red Sammy as "the Devil or his agent" and thus The Tower as a kind of hell, The Misfit as Death and "an existential Everyman," his forgotten crime as original sin). Marks's allegorizing, however, is flexible enough to allow for interesting comments on such varied matters as the pursuits of pleasure on this vacation trip, the role of time and chance, and the significance of the story of Mr. Teagarden and the watermelon.

Marks discusses the climax of "A Good Man"—the grandmother's reaching out to The Misfit and his shooting of her—only from the perspective of The Misfit. It was Brainard Cheney (like Gordon, another friend of O'Connor's) who first called the grandmother's words and gesture her acceptance of "the charity of salvation" ("Miss O'Connor Creates Unusual Humor Out of Ordinary Sin," 1963). This reading was repeated, and underlined by a letter of O'Connor's authorizing such an interpretation, in the initial book-length study of her work, Carter Martin's *The True Country: Themes in the Fiction of Flannery O'Connor* (1969). Within a year, however, Josephine Hendin (*The World of Flannery O'Connor*) had mounted the first attack on this way of reading the story. Contrasting the emotional and symbolic flatness of O'Connor's fiction with the mythic sense found in other Southerners such as William Faulkner and William Styron, Hendin's antitheological analysis stresses the "feeling of undifferentiated life—of there being few distinctions between living and dying" conveyed by "A Good Man." O'Connor probably meant The Misfit to be "a kind of Christ," Hendin says, but the grandmother also tries to be *his* redeemer, and the result is that they are "crucifying *each other*." What O'Connor presents, she argues, is not the possibility of transcendence, but rather "the horror . . . at the core of family life."

If there were no immediate follow-ups to Hendin's challenge, one important reason was the appearance in 1969 of O'Connor's collected non-fictional prose, *Mystery and Manners,* which contained her own introductory comments to "A Good Man." Much of the thematic criticism that followed presented elaborations of this authorial version of the story. In *The Eternal Crossroads* (1971), Leon V. Driskell and Joan T. Brittain's most significant contribution is to show how the issues raised in this tale are varied throughout the stories collected in *A Good Man Is Hard to Find* until a genuine "good man" is discovered in the last one, "The Displaced Person." Kathleen Feeley (*Flannery O'Connor: Voice of the Peacock,* 1972) stresses the confrontation at the center of the story between romanticist and agnostic and argues that it is "vision" that returns the first to "reality," while rationalism allows the latter only a very literal view of it. Gilbert Muller's *Nightmares and Visions* (1972) shows how various aspects of "A Good Man" are related to the grotesque, and David Eggenschwiler uses Kierkegaard's concept of "demonic man" to show how psychological and spiritual approaches to The Misfit might be reconciled (*The Christian Humanism of Flannery O'Connor,* 1972). Published the same year, Miles Orvell's *Invisible Parade* points out the recurrence of a favorite O'Connor motif in the grandmother's dreamy desire for "home," arguing that the "violent logic" of The Misfit in its demands of "total commitment" is (*pace* Eggenschwiler) a denial of humanism.

Up to this time, "A Good Man" had been implicitly accepted as a successfully executed story, the only qualification being that brief criticism of the handling of point of view from Gordon and Tate. Dissent from this favorable evaluation arises, again, on technical grounds. William S. Doxey finds the story seriously flawed by a *change* in point of view from the grandmother to The Misfit, a switch that he conjectures was brought about by O'Connor's theological emphasis, her insistence on making The Misfit the agent of grace ("A Dissenting Opinion of Flannery O'Connor's 'A Good Man Is Hard to Find,'" 1973). Writing at almost the same time, Martha Stephens also raises questions about a shift midway through the story, although for her this involves a radical change not in point of view, but in tone (*The Question of Flannery O'Connor,* 1973). Stephens discusses at length the comedy of the first part of the story which, she argues, suddenly and inappropriately gives way to the grim painfulness of the latter portion. Like Doxey, Stephens attributes this disturbing shift to O'Connor's doctrinal concerns.

Preston Browning's *Flannery O'Connor* (1974) is most illuminating on the echoes of Dostoyevsky in The Misfit's dilemma and on the moral complexity of his position. In *The Pruning Word* (1976) John R. May argues specifically against Stephens's reading. In the course of his treatment of the work as a "parable," he points out those dark and ironic suggestions in the first part of the story that for him deny any radical shift in tone. However, most other discussions of this period stress the story's thematic—and especially theological—concerns, often, like Marion Montgomery in *Why Flannery O'Connor Stayed Home* (1981), enlarging on the author's own comments. Michael O. Bellamy, however, challenges O'Connor's avowed Catholicism by arguing that "A Good Man" more convincingly dramatizes a Protestant form of grace, faith, and election ("Everything Off Balance: Protestant Election in Flannery O'Connor's 'A Good Man Is Hard to Find,'" 1979). And as his title suggests Richard Giannone's *Flannery O'Connor and the Mystery of Love* (1989) explores the divine love that produces the grandmother's goodness.

Meanwhile, more specific aspects of the story began to get investigated. Two essays, J. O. Tate's "A Good Source Is Not So Hard to Find" (1980) and Victor Lasseter's "The Genesis of Flannery O'Connor's 'A Good Man Is Hard to Find" (1982), uncover newspaper sources for the character of The Misfit—his name, his politeness, his henchmen, the prison escape, the ensuing crime wave. Hallman B. Bryant, by "Reading the Map in 'A Good Man Is Hard to Find'" (1981), discovers not only O'Connor's use of the actual geography of Georgia, but also the limits of such local realism, her departures from it in order to include the out-of-the-way Stone Mountain and the non-existent Timothy, which turns out to be an allusion rather than a town. One can make too much of this, but to be reminded that the story has one foot firmly planted in the world of local geography and journalistic reportage seems a healthy corrective to the theological bent of so much criticism of "A Good Man."

As the 1980s progressed, there were several attempts to gain a fresh perspective on the story. Frederick Asals's *Flannery O'Connor: The Imagination of Extremity* (1982) focuses on the dramatically broken action created by the car accident in order to investigate the resulting incongruities. In "'The Meanest of Them Sparkled': Beauty and Landscape in Flannery O'Connor's Fiction" (1987), Carter Martin draws attention to the neglected sense of beauty to be found in "A Good Man." Edward Kessler (*Flannery O'Connor and the Language of Apocalypse,* 1986) analyses the use of *as if* constructions as a means of unfixing rather than clarifying meaning, of throwing everything "off balance." Two essays, rather than treating O'Connor in isolation, speak of her affinities with and possible debts to other writers and works. William J. Scheick ("Flannery O'Connor's 'A Good Man Is Hard to Find' and G. K. Chesterton's *Manalive,*" 1983) suggests not only a source for the story but also ways in which O'Connor may have revised the vision of her fellow-Catholic. J. Peter Dyson, following up the name of the grandmother's cat, shows how astonishingly rich such an unlikely source as Gilbert and Sullivan can be for this story ("Cats, Crime, and Punishment: *The Mikado*'s Pitti-Sing in 'A Good Man Is Hard to Find,'" 1988). And in a nuanced essay, O'Connor's fellow fiction writer Madison Jones assesses "A Good Man's Predicament" (1984), shedding new light on the vexed question of the story's climactic moments.

Around the same time, some of the newer critical approaches to literature known as "structuralist" and "post-structuralist" began to make themselves apparent in studies of O'Connor. Differing and even antagonistic as some of these theories are, they have in common—and share with New Criticism—a dedication to close attention to the language of the literary text, the insistence that whatever else a story may be, it is first of all a creation in *words*. Thus the French critic Claude Richard ("Désir et Destin dans 'A Good Man Is Hard to Find,'" 1976) looks closely not only at the language of the story, but at the grandmother's *reliance* on words in order to distinguish the "cultural" from the "natural" and to trace her movement from the former to the latter. Mary Jane Schenck's "Deconstructed Meaning in Two Short Stories by Flannery O'Connor" (1988) draws on theories of Paul de Man to argue that his notion of the creation of a second "self" out of language is related to O'Connor's use of irony. In Schenck's reading, "A Good Man" gives us not only the confrontation between the grandmother and The Misfit, but between a self based on sense-knowledge and a self constructed from language in each of the antagonists. Two recent critics have employed the insights of the Russian theorist Mikhail Bakhtin. Marshall Bruce Gentry (*Flannery O'Connor's Religion of the Grotesque*, 1986) was the first to apply to O'Connor's fiction Bakhtin's notion of "dialogism"—the sense that no speech act is really simple (or "monologic"), that language is always involved with interchange and interaction, with other utterances, others' words—and Gentry reads "A Good Man" as acting out a redemption of the narrator from a "monologic" stance at the start of the story. Similarly, for Robert H. Brinkmeyer, Jr. in *The Art and Vision of Flannery O'Connor* (1989), The Misfit's dialogue challenges not only the clichés of the grandmother, but the faith of the author—not just her acknowledged Catholicism, but the fundamentalist Protestant strain in her Christianity as well. It seems safe to predict that new readings of "A Good Man Is Hard to Find" will not end here.

Feminist criticism has not found Flannery O'Connor in general, and "A Good Man" in particular, congenial territory. In the most extensive such study to date, *Sacred Groves and Ravaged Gardens* (1985), Louise Westling juxtaposes O'Connor with fellow Southerners Eudora Welty and Carson McCullers and not surprisingly finds her treatment of typical female themes and motifs the least traditional of these writers, particularly in her refusal to espouse values usually associated with women.[9] Westling mentions "A Good Man" only in passing, and when we reflect on the story's central character, it does not seem hard to see why it has lacked for feminist attention.

III

Since the "Background to the Story" contains two of O'Connor's own anecdotes about the reactions of undergraduate students to "A Good Man," it may not be inappropriate to add a third. Granted, these were not Southern students like those O'Connor was sure "all had grandmothers or great-aunts just like [the story's protagonist] at home"; my students were Canadian, and they were not at all convinced that this "old lady . . . had a good heart." They found this central female character not only "a hypocritical old soul," but the possessor of assorted juicy sins unforgivable to the minds of nineteen-year-olds—garrulous, insensitive, underhanded, pretentious, manipulative, self-serving, morally obtuse, out of touch with "reality," and so on. In short, they *judged* the grandmother, and they did so in part because they felt, and not incorrectly, that the story invited such judgment; they sensed, even if they could not always articulate it, the narrator's ironic tone, the element of caricature in the presentation (nor were they blind to the bratty children, the lumpish mother, the sullen father in this family). And if they were puzzled by the import of her last words to The Misfit and somewhat shaken by the wholesale massacre in the final part of the story, they did not find this old lady's demise entirely without moral justification. The wind moving through the trees "like a long satisfied insuck of breath" as the gunshots go off seems an expressive summation of their response.

Surely an important part of the story's effectiveness, of the pleasure we are able to take in what, outlined, would seem merely grim tabloid material, comes from such stylization, from the ironic comedy which distances the reader from this family and particularly from its chief member, the grandmother. Nevertheless, she is the "chief member" only because the story has so presented her, privileging her point of view over that of the others. Within the family itself, she is clearly a marginal figure, ignored (as we see in the opening scene) by her son and daughter-in-law, freely insulted by her grandchildren, powerless before all. If she is all the things my students claimed, surely that is because she has to be: her comically desperate attempts to assert a self that is denied by all around her, no less by the parents' silence than by the children's diminishing taunts ("She has to go everywhere we go"), testify to her lack of any essential role in the only context which age, sex, and widowhood have left open to her.

Failing to produce even a reconsideration of family vacation plans, she apparently capitulates with absurd rapidity: "The next morning the grandmother was the first one in the car, ready to go" (as the children claim, she is not about to be left behind, and she doubtless considers promptness a cardinal virtue). Nonetheless, the hidden presence of her cat, Pitty Sing, suggests a more complex response. Her reasons for taking the animal expose both her sentimentality and that melodramatic imagination which has already drawn her to newspaper reports of The Misfit—"he would miss her too much and she was afraid he might brush against one of the gas burners and accidentally asphyxiate himself"—but the paragraph's final sentence, which concerns not the inclusion but the secreting of Pitty Sing, hints at something more. "Her son, Bailey, didn't like to arrive at a motel with a cat" presents the animal as agent of rebellion, the grandmother's private refusal to acquiesce without at least a token of revolt against an order that denies her. If she has her way, Bailey *will,* like it or not, "arrive at a motel with a cat."

No such destination, of course, is ever reached, but the cat nevertheless plays a key role in the story's action. By that time, however, it has become a more problematic locus of possibilities. The grandmother has spun her tale of the plantation house, and for once, backed by the children (who first said grandparents and grandchildren naturally gravitate together to face a common enemy?), she has apparently finally got her way, moved the family in the direction of her desires. That archetypal Southern mansion both has and is a pseudo-secret—the grandmother knows there is no hidden panel in the house, and she is about to discover there is no house at all down that road—and with the sudden revelation to her of the truth, she uncovers the genuine secret of the cat. "The thought was so embarrassing that she turned red in the face and her eyes dilated and her feet jumped up, upsetting her valise in the corner. The instant the valise moved, the newspaper top she had over the basket rose with a snarl and Pitty Sing, the cat, sprang onto Bailey's shoulder." The cat, like The

Misfit, identified through their common "snarl," will not be contained by the newspaper, and as a result the car flips over into a ditch.

This is the turning point of "A Good Man," the "ACCIDENT" that occurs precisely at the story's half-way mark. It is the moment in the tale that novelist T. Coraghessan Boyle recently approved because it "violate[s] the familiar comic balance": "It's very powerful when the safety net drops away from the comic universe where nothing can go wrong, and there's this overpowering, terrible violence."[10] The sudden, unpredictable quality of the car accident is essential to the effect and implications of "A Good Man," yet so is the recognition that it has been precipitated, however obliquely, by the grandmother. But if her original smuggling aboard of the cat suggested her underground revolt against the family's suppression, the uncovering of that secret seems to imply a different focus of dissatisfaction. Despite the fact that Pitty Sing springs directly at Bailey, patriarch of the new order that diminishes her, the grandmother's release of the cat results from her visceral acknowledgement of her *own* failure, of the falsity of that sentimental symbol of the old order she believes she believes in, the plantation house. The cat thus comprehends the rejection of *both* social orders, the old and the new, as somehow inadequate; both Florida and the plantation house fail as possible destinations. If the story provides no justification for the grandmother's sentimental concern that the cat "would miss her too much" (note its final appearance in the closing paragraphs), it abundantly justifies her belief in a fatally melodramatic world where "he might *accidentally* asphyxiate himself" [italics added].

That world is most fully defined in the story by The Misfit, whom the accident seems to conjure up, as if the very incarnation of such a universe. His self-chosen title, he tells us, proclaims both his recognition of this world and his place in it, a paradoxically inevitable existence of radical contingency where "one is punished a heap and another ain't punished at all." I have argued elsewhere that while The Misfit claims to have lived this experience, the story in its very structure demonstrates it, breaking its action with the car accident and bringing down on all members of this family, even to the infant, the same lethal "punishment." Yet, in her heart of hearts, the grandmother recognizes this world too, even to the point of absurdly dressing for it. She is carefully groomed so that "In case of an *accident*, anyone seeing her dead on the highway would know at once that she was a lady" [italics added]. In short, the gap between the grandmother and The Misfit, which closes with her fatal recognition of him as "one of my babies . . . one of my own children," is never as great as it may at first appear.

Nevertheless, the action of the story is precisely designed to uncover this awareness in her, to apply such pressure that all her unquestioned assumptions will be gradually denied until her physical collapse in the ditch manifests the loss of her accustomed inner supports. It is The Misfit's stripping away of her "social" ("good blood," "nice people"), materialistic ("You must have stolen something"), and conventionally religious (If you would pray . . . Jesus would help you") values that brings the grandmother to her moment of recognition, yet both the presence of the cat and the occasion of its catastrophic leap imply her readiness to undertake and respond to this cathartic process: the purging of the values both of a contemporary world which allows her no role and a nostalgic one which has built for her only a hollow, inauthentic self.

Meanwhile, her male antagonist is undergoing an analogous process whereby his apparent self-sufficiency and command is gradually revealed as a form of armor, a veneer which falls away to uncover the "baby" with a gun. For all the backwoods *politesse* and homemade existentialism which locate him in this particular time and place, The Misfit is in essence a variation on that enduring American type, the individualistic male whose violence both expresses and substitutes for inner incompleteness. Despite his assertion, he is not "doing all right by myself," but the only "hep" he might accept would be disembodied, intellectual—to have "known" whether or not Jesus raised the dead so that "I wouldn't be," as he at last admits, "like I am now." The messiness and disorder of life in the flesh, particularly the domestic flesh, is anathema to him: children make him "nervous," and the touch of a foolish old woman who sees him momentarily as "one of my children" triggers a visceral, defensive violence. If, as O'Connor said, "It is the extreme situation that best reveals what we are essentially," what is revealed in The Misfit is an anger and anguish never entirely assuaged by the "meanness" he visits on the world around him.

And what is revealed about the grandmother in *her* comparable moment of extremity? Taking the identification of The Misfit as "one of my babies" together with the gesture of reaching out to him as O'Connor says she intended us to, we can see the grandmother adopting for the first time an archetypal female role, one that she has denied, but that has also been denied her, in the family context so fiercely limned in the earlier part of the story. If we wish to press that maternal gesture in the direction of O'Connor's declared Catholicism, we can see glimmer through the grandmother the figure of the Grand Mother, a momentary *imitatio Virginis*—Our Lady of Sorrows, the Hope of Criminals, and so on. However, as other critics have shown, if we ignore O'Connor's comments, it seems possible to see this as one last self-serving grasp at survival, or as an ironically threatening identification (all her other "children" are dead), or as an attempt to "adopt" The Misfit into her smothering, diminishing superficiality.

But the story itself has more to say of the grandmother: two other roles here get pressed on her in a kind of double epitaph, one by The Misfit, the other by the narrator. Her corpse is described with its legs crossed under it "like a child's and her face smiling up at the cloudless sky" just before The Misfit pronounces, "She would of been a good woman . . . if it had been somebody there to shoot her every minute of her life." Both "child" and "woman," of course, ignore the grandmother's own social self-identification, "lady," and at first appear so antithetically matched as to raise the suspicion of irony. The dissonance may at first seem reconcilable by noting the gap between the living and the dead, between childlike corpse and living "woman"—until we realize that both designations must be applied to the very moment before death. We can, with a small stretch, give the passage a Christian reading in which the grandmother, stripped to her essential being as a genuine "woman," has, in her recovery of simplicity, become again as a little child. Yet it can also be understood more darkly, to suggest that the recovery of one's genuine female self is a dangerous business indeed, likely to reduce one to a condition of double and final powerlessness, the child-like corpse.

However we interpret the ending of "A Good Man," or indeed the tale as a whole, it seems to go on resonating in the imagination, perhaps the single story that has most compellingly captured that condition of modern American life where, in Boyle's words, "the safety net drops away" and we are suddenly confronted with an overwhelming violence, a violence that apparently chooses its victims randomly and before which they are helpless. That sense of impotence in the face of terror is the stuff of nightmares (one might note that, with terror lightened to "unpleasantness," it is also the stuff of the grandmother's daily life in the earlier part of the story), and as such it addresses some of our deepest fears. Such fears, as "A Good Man" itself implies, are hardly peculiar to women, yet it seems inevitable that the protagonist of such a story should be female, and that the prolonged confrontation with an armed male should end in her death. This much is all too familiar, yet O'Connor would have us note not simply the man's violent gesture—"The Misfit sprang back . . . and shot her three times through the chest"—but also the woman's motions, particularly those with which she begins and ends. Her opening gesture is an aggressive (but useless) "rattling the newspaper" at the bald head of "her only boy," who continues to ignore her; her final one is to reach out and touch on the shoulder the man she calls "one of my own children." He will certainly not ignore her, but the distance she has travelled in these twenty-odd pages places her with the figures of classic American stories—from Irving's Ichabod Crane, Melville's Benito Cereno, and Stephen Crane's Swede to those of Flannery O'Connor's contemporaries, Eudora Welty's Clytie, J. D. Salinger's Teddy, Ralph Ellison's "King of the Bingo Game"—whose initiations into a frightening world are both astonishing and lethal.

Notes

1. Sally Fitzgerald, ed., *The Habit of Being: Letters of Flannery O'Connor* (New York: Farrar, Straus and Giroux, 1979), 542. Future citations from this source will be included parenthetically in the text preceded by *Habit*.

2. William Phillips and Philip Rahv, eds., *Modern Writing 1* (New York: Avon Publications, 1953), 186–199. The major difference between this version of "A Good Man Is Hard to Find" and the one that appeared in the 1955 collection is that the turn-off onto a dirt road and all that follows from it is the result of a detour necessitated by road construction; the grandmother's recollection of the plantation house, the "secret panel," and the deliberate turn-around to take the dirt road appear for the first time in *A Good Man Is Hard to Find and Other Stories*.

3. Flannery O'Connor, *Everything That Rises Must Converge* (New York: Farrar, Straus and Giroux, 1965), xxvi. Fitzgerald wrote the introduction to this posthumously published collection.

4. The letter is undated, but its reference to the Brainard Cheneys' coming "into the Church the Saturday before" indicates that O'Connor's letter to the Fitzgeralds closely follows the Cheneys' March 22 letter to her informing her of that event. See *The Corre-*

spondence of Flannery O'Connor and the Brainard Cheneys, ed. C. Ralph Stephens (Jackson and London: University Press of Mississippi, 1986), 4–5.

5. The title of the story, as well as being a cliché, is also the title of a song, an older one than "The Tennessee Waltz." Perhaps appropriately, it is a blues number.

6. Caroline Gordon and Allen Tate, eds., *The House of Fiction* (New York: Charles Scribner's Sons, 1960). Page references will be included parenthetically within the text.

7. Melvin J. Friedman and Lewis A. Lawson, eds., *The Added Dimension: The Art and Mind of Flannery O'Connor* (New York: Fordham University Press, 1966), 135.

8. Critical works mentioned in the introduction but not included in this volume have been cited either in the bibliography or in the notes to the introduction.

9. Louise Westling, *Sacred Groves and Damaged Gardens: The Fiction of Eudora Welty, Carson McCullers, and Flannery O'Connor* (Athens: University of Georgia Press, 1985).

10. Boyle is quoted by Tad Friend in "Rolling Boyle," *The New York Times Magazine,* 9 December 1990, p. 50.

Chronology

1925	Born Mary Flannery O'Connor in Savannah, Georgia, March 25.
1938	O'Connor family moves to Milledgeville.
1945	B.A. from the Georgia State College for Women in Milledgeville.
1947	M.F.A. from Writers' Workshop, University of Iowa.
1948–50	At Yaddo, New York City, and Connecticut.
1951	Dangerously ill with lupus, takes up permanent residence in Milledgeville.
1952	Publication of *Wise Blood.*
1953	"A Good Man Is Hard to Find" published in *Modern Writing I.*
1955	Publication of *A Good Man Is Hard to Find and Other Stories.*
1960	Publication of *The Violent Bear It Away.*
1964	Dies in Milledgeville, August 3.
1965	Publication of *Everything That Rises Must Converge.*
1988	*Collected Works* published by The Library of America.

A Good Man Is Hard to Find

A Good Man Is Hard to Find

The grandmother didn't want to go to Florida. She wanted to visit some of her connections in east Tennessee and she was seizing at every chance to change Bailey's mind. Bailey was the son she lived with, her only boy. He was sitting on the edge of his chair at the table, bent over the orange sports section of the *Journal*. "Now look here, Bailey," she said, "see here, read this," and she stood with one hand on her thin hip and the other rattling the newspaper at his bald head. "Here this fellow that calls himself The Misfit is aloose from the Federal Pen and headed toward Florida and you read here what it says he did to these people. Just you read it. I wouldn't take my children in any direction with a criminal like that aloose in it. I couldn't answer to my conscience if I did."

Bailey didn't look up from his reading so she wheeled around then and faced the children's mother, a young woman in slacks, whose face was as broad and

---

From *A Good Man Is Hard to Find and Other Stories* by Flannery O'Connor (New York: Harcourt, Brace and Company, 1955), 9–29. Seen through the press by O'Connor, this is the most reliable version of the story; the posthumous *Complete Stories* silently corrects The Misfit's dialect (e.g., "thown" becomes "thrown").

innocent as a cabbage and was tied around with a green head-kerchief that had two points on the top like rabbit's ears. She was sitting on the sofa, feeding the baby his apricots out of a jar. "The children have been to Florida before," the old lady said. "You all ought to take them somewhere else for a change so they would see different parts of the world and be broad. They never have been to east Tennessee."

The children's mother didn't seem to hear her but the eight-year-old boy, John Wesley, a stocky child with glasses, said, "If you don't want to go to Florida, why dontcha stay at home?" He and the little girl, June Star, were reading the funny papers on the floor.

"She wouldn't stay at home to be queen for a day," June Star said without raising her yellow head.

"Yes and what would you do if this fellow, The Misfit, caught you?" the grandmother asked.

"I'd smack his face," John Wesley said.

"She wouldn't stay at home for a million bucks," June Star said. "Afraid she'd miss something. She has to go everywhere we go."

"All right, Miss," the grandmother said. "Just remember that the next time you want me to curl your hair."

June Star said her hair was naturally curly.

The next morning the grandmother was the first one in the car, ready to go. She had her big black valise that looked like the head of a hippopotamus in one corner, and underneath it she was hiding a basket with Pitty Sing, the cat, in it. She didn't intend for the cat to be left alone in the house for three days because he would miss her too much and she was afraid he might brush against one of her gas burners and accidentally asphyxiate himself. Her son, Bailey, didn't like to arrive at a motel with a cat.

She sat in the middle of the back seat with John Wesley and June Star on either side of her. Bailey and the children's mother and the baby sat in front and they left Atlanta at eight forty-five with the mileage on the car at 55890. The grandmother wrote this down because she thought it would be interesting to say how many miles they had been when they got back. It took them twenty minutes to reach the outskirts of the city.

The old lady settled herself comfortably, removing her white cotton gloves and putting them up with her purse on the shelf in front of the back window. The children's mother still had on slacks and still had her head tied up in a green kerchief, but the grandmother had on a navy blue straw sailor hat with a bunch of white violets on the brim and a navy blue dress with a small white dot in the print. Her collars and cuffs were white organdy trimmed with lace and at her neckline she had pinned a purple spray of cloth violets containing a sachet. In case of an accident, anyone seeing her dead on the highway would know at once that she was a lady.

She said she thought it was going to be a good day for driving, neither too hot nor too cold, and she cautioned Bailey that the speed limit was fifty-five miles an hour and that the patrolmen hid themselves behind billboards and small clumps of trees and sped out after you before you had a chance to slow down. She pointed out interesting details of the scenery: Stone Mountain; the blue granite that in some places came up to both sides of the highway; the brilliant red clay banks slightly streaked with purple; and the various crops that made rows of green lace-work on the ground. The trees were full of silver-white sunlight and the meanest of them sparkled. The children were reading comic magazines and their mother and gone back to sleep.

"Let's go through Georgia fast so we won't have to look at it much," John Wesley said.

"If I were a little boy," said the grandmother, "I wouldn't talk about my native state that way. Tennessee has the mountains and Georgia has the hills."

"Tennessee is just a hillbilly dumping ground," John Wesley said, "and Georgia is a lousy state too."

"You said it," June Star said.

"In my time," said the grandmother, folding her thin veined fingers, "children were more respectful of their native states and their parents and everything else. People did right then. Oh look at the cute little pickaninny!" she said and pointed to a Negro child standing in the door of a shack. "Wouldn't that make a picture, now?" she asked and they all turned and looked at the little Negro out of the back window. He waved.

"He didn't have any britches on," June Star said.

"He probably didn't have any," the grandmother explained. "Little niggers in the country don't have things like we do. If I could paint, I'd paint that picture," she said.

The children exchanged comic books.

The grandmother offered to hold the baby and the children's mother passed him over the front seat to her. She set him on her knee and bounced him and told him about the things they were passing. She rolled her eyes and screwed up her mouth and stuck her leathery thin face into his smooth bland one. Occasionally he gave her a faraway smile. They passed a large cotton field with five or fix graves fenced in the middle of it, like a small island. "Look at the graveyard!" the grandmother said, pointing it out. "That was the old family burying ground. That belonged to the plantation."

"Where's the plantation?" John Wesley asked.

"Gone With the Wind," said the grandmother. "Ha. Ha."

When the children finished all the comic books they had brought, they opened the lunch and ate it. The grandmother ate a peanut butter sandwich and an olive and would not let the children throw the box and the paper napkins out the window. When there was nothing else to do they played a game by choosing a cloud and making the other two guess what shape it suggested. John Wesley took one the shape of a cow and June Star guessed a cow and John Wesley said, no, an automobile, and June Star said he didn't play fair, and they began to slap each other over the grandmother.

The grandmother said she would tell them a story if they would keep quiet. When she told a story, she rolled her eyes and waved her head and was very dramatic. She said once when she was a maiden lady she had been courted by a Mr. Edgar Atkins Teagarden from Jasper, Georgia. She said he was a very good-looking man and a gentleman and that he brought her a watermelon every Saturday afternoon with his initials cut in it, E. A. T. Well, one Saturday, she said, Mr. Teagarden brought the watermelon and there was nobody at home and he left it on the front porch and returned in his buggy to Jasper, but she never got the watermelon, she said, because a nigger boy ate it when he saw the initials, E. A. T.! This story tickled John Wesley's funny bone and he giggled and giggled but June Star didn't think it was any good. She said she wouldn't marry a man that just brought her a watermelon on Saturday. The grandmother said she would have done well to marry Mr. Teagarden because he was a gentleman and had bought Coca-Cola stock when it first came out and that he had died only a few years ago, a very wealthy man.

They stopped at The Tower for barbecued sandwiches. The Tower was a part stucco and part wood filling station and dance hall set in a clearing outside of Timothy. A fat man named Red Sammy Butts ran it and there were signs stuck here and there on the building and for miles up and down the highway saying, TRY RED SAMMY'S FAMOUS BARBECUE. NONE LIKE FAMOUS RED SAMMY'S! RED SAM! THE FAT BOY WITH THE HAPPY LAUGH. A VETERAN! RED SAMMY'S YOUR MAN!

Red Sammy was lying on the bare ground outside The Tower with his head under a truck while a gray monkey about a foot high, chained to a small chinaberry tree, chattered nearby. The monkey sprang back into the tree and got on the highest limb as soon as he saw the children jump out of the car and run toward him.

Inside, The Tower was a long dark room with a counter at one end and tables at the other and dancing space in the middle. They all sat down at a board table next to the nickelodeon and Red Sam's wife, a tall burnt-brown woman with hair and eyes lighter than her skin, came and took their order. The children's mother put a dime in the machine and played "The Tennessee Waltz," and the grandmother said that tune always made her want to dance. She asked Bailey if he would like to dance but he only glared at her. He didn't have a naturally sunny disposition like she did and trips made him nervous. The grandmother's brown eyes were very bright. She swayed her head from side to side and pretended she was dancing in her chair. June Star said play something she could tap to so the children's mother put in another dime and played a fast number and June Star stepped out onto the dance floor and did her tap routine.

"Ain't she cute?" Red Sam's wife said, leaning over the counter. "Would you like to come be my little girl?"

"No I certainly wouldn't," June Star said. "I wouldn't live in a broken-down place like this for a million bucks!" and she ran back to the table.

"Ain't she cute?" the woman repeated, stretching her mouth politely.

"Arn't you ashamed?" hissed the grandmother.

Red Sam came in and told his wife to quit lounging on the counter and hurry up with these people's order. His khaki trousers reached just to his hip bones and his stomach hung over them like a sack of meal swaying under his shirt. He came over and sat down at a table nearby and let out a combination sigh and yodel. "You can't win," he said. "You can't win," and he wiped his sweating red face off with a gray handkerchief. "These days you don't know who to trust," he said. "Ain't that the truth?"

"People are certainly not nice like they used to be," said the grandmother.

"Two fellers come in here last week," Red Sammy said, "driving a Chrysler. It was a old beat-up car but it was a good one and these boys looked all right to me. Said they worked at the mill and you know I let them fellers charge the gas they bought? Now why did I do that?"

"Because you're a good man!" the grandmother said at once.

"Yes'm, I suppose so," Red Sam said as if he were struck with this answer.

His wife brought the orders, carrying the five

plates all at once without a tray, two in each hand and one balanced on her arm. "It isn't a soul in this green world of God's that you can trust," she said. "And I don't count nobody out of that, not nobody," she repeated, looking at Red Sammy.

"Did you read about that criminal, The Misfit, that's escaped?" asked the grandmother.

"I wouldn't be a bit surprised if he didn't attact this place right here," said the woman. "If he hears about it being here, I wouldn't be none surprised to see him. If he hears it's two cent in the cash register, I wouldn't be a tall surprised if he . . ."

"That'll do," Red Sam said. "Go bring these people their Co'-Colas," and the woman went off to get the rest of the order.

"A good man is hard to find," Red Sammy said. "Everything is getting terrible. I remember the day you could go off and leave your screen door unlatched. Not no more."

He and the grandmother discussed better times. The old lady said that in her opinion Europe was entirely to blame for the way things were now. She said the way Europe acted you would think we were made of money and Red Sam said it was no use talking about it, she was exactly right. The children ran outside into the white sunlight and looked at the monkey in the lacy chinaberry tree. He was busy catching fleas on himself and biting each one carefully between his teeth as if it were a delicacy.

They drove off again into the hot afternoon. The grandmother took cat naps and woke up every few minutes with her own snoring. Outside of Toombsboro she woke up and recalled an old plantation that she had visited in this neighborhood once when she was a young lady. She said the house had six white columns across the front and that there was an avenue of oaks leading up to it and two little wooden trellis arbors on either side in front where you sat down with your suitor after a stroll in the garden. She recalled exactly which road to turn off to get to it. She knew that Bailey would not be willing to lose any time looking at an old house, but the more she talked about it, the more she wanted to see it once again and find out if the little twin arbors were still standing. "There was a secret panel in this house," she said craftily, not telling the truth but wishing that she were, "and the story went that all the family silver was hidden in it when Sherman came through but it was never found . . ."

"Hey!" John Wesley said. "Let's go see it! We'll find it! We'll poke all the woodwork and find it! Who lives there? Where do you turn off at? Hey Pop, can't we turn off there?"

"We never have seen a house with a secret panel!" June Star shrieked. "Let's go to the house with the secret panel! Hey Pop, can't we go see the house with the secret panel!"

"It's not far from here, I know," the grandmother said. "It wouldn't take over twenty minutes."

Bailey was looking straight ahead. His jaw was as rigid as a horseshoe. "No," he said.

The children began to yell and scream that they wanted to see the house with the secret panel. John Wesley kicked the back of the front seat and June Star hung over her mother's shoulder and whined desperately into her ear that they never had any fun even on their vacation, that they could never do what THEY wanted to do. The baby began to scream and John Wesley kicked the back of the seat so hard that his father could feel the blows in his kidney.

"All right!" he shouted and drew the car to a stop

at the side of the road. "Will you all shut up? Will you all just shut up for one second? If you don't shut up, we won't go anywhere."

"It would be very educational for them," the grandmother murmured.

"All right," Bailey said, "but get this: this is the only time we're going to stop for anything like this. This is the one and only time."

"The dirt road that you have to turn down is about a mile back," the grandmother directed. "I marked it when we passed."

"A dirt road," Bailey groaned.

After they had turned around and were headed toward the dirt road, the grandmother recalled other points about the house, the beautiful glass over the front doorway and the candle-lamp in the hall. John Wesley said that the secret panel was probably in the fireplace.

"You can't go inside this house," Bailey said. "You don't know who lives there."

"While you all talk to the people in front, I'll run around behind and get in a window," John Wesley suggested.

"We'll all stay in the car," his mother said.

They turned onto the dirt road and the car raced roughly along in a swirl of pink dust. The grandmother recalled the times when there were no paved roads and thirty miles was a day's journey. The dirt road was hilly and there were sudden washes in it and sharp curves on dangerous embankments. All at once they would be on a hill, looking down over the blue tops of trees for miles around, then the next minute, they would be in a red depression with the dust-coated trees looking down on them.

"This place had better turn up in a minute," Bailey said, "or I'm going to turn around."

The road looked as if no one had traveled on it in months.

"It's not much farther," the grandmother said and just as she said it, a horrible thought came to her. The thought was so embarrassing that she turned red in the face and her eyes dilated and her feet jumped up, upsetting her valise in the corner. The instant the valise moved, the newspaper top she had over the basket under it rose with a snarl and Pitty Sing, the cat, sprang onto Bailey's shoulder.

The children were thrown to the floor and their mother, clutching the baby, was thrown out the door onto the ground; the old lady was thrown into the front seat. The car turned over once and landed right-side-up in a gulch off the side of the road. Bailey remained in the driver's seat with the cat—gray-striped with a broad white face and an orange nose—clinging to his neck like a caterpillar.

As soon as the children saw they could move their arms and legs, they scrambled out of the car, shouting, "We've had an ACCIDENT!" The grandmother was curled up under the dashboard, hoping she was injured so that Bailey's wrath would not come down on her all at once. The horrible thought she had had before the accident was that the house she had remembered so vividly was not in Georgia but in Tennessee.

Bailey removed the cat from his neck with both hands and flung it out the window against the side of a pine tree. Then he got out of the car and started looking for the children's mother. She was sitting against the side of the red gutted ditch, holding the screaming baby, but she only had a cut down her face and a broken shoulder. "We've had an ACCIDENT!" the children screamed in a frenzy of delight.

"But nobody's killed," June Star said with disappointment as the grandmother limped out of the car, her hat still pinned to her head but the broken front brim standing up at a jaunty angle and the violet spray hanging off the side. They all sat down in the ditch, except the children, to recover from the shock. They were all shaking.

"Maybe a car will come along," said the children's mother hoarsely.

"I believe I have injured an organ," said the grandmother, pressing her side, but no one answered her. Bailey's teeth were clattering. He had on a yellow sport shirt with bright blue parrots designed in it and his face was as yellow as the shirt. The grandmother decided that she would not mention that the house was in Tennessee.

The road was about ten feet above and they could see only the tops of the trees on the other side of it. Behind the ditch they were sitting in there were more woods, tall and dark and deep. In a few minutes they saw a car some distance away on top of a hill, coming slowly as if the occupants were watching them. The grandmother stood up and waved both arms dramatically to attract their attention. The car continued to come on slowly, disappeared around a bend and appeared again, moving even slower, on top of the hill they had gone over. It was a big black battered hearse-like automobile. There were three men in it.

It came to a stop just over them and for some minutes, the driver looked down with a steady expressionless gaze to where they were sitting, and didn't speak. Then he turned his head and muttered something to the other two and they got out. One was a fat boy in black trousers and a red sweat shirt with a silver stallion embossed on the front of it. He moved around on the right side of them and stood staring, his mouth partly open in a kind of loose grin. The other had on khaki pants and a blue striped coat and a gray hat pulled down very low, hiding most of his face. He came around slowly on the left side. Neither spoke.

The driver got out of the car and stood by the side of it, looking down at them. He was an older man than the other two. His hair was just beginning to gray and he wore silver-rimmed spectacles that gave him a scholarly look. He had a long creased face and didn't have on any shirt or undershirt. He had on blue jeans that were too tight for him and was holding a black hat and a gun. The two boys also had guns.

"We've had an ACCIDENT!" the children screamed.

The grandmother had the peculiar feeling that the bespectacled man was someone she knew. His face was as familiar to her as if she had known him all her life but she could not recall who he was. He moved away from the car and began to come down the embankment, placing his feet carefully so that he wouldn't slip. He had on tan and white shoes and no socks, and his ankles were red and thin. "Good afternoon," he said. "I see you all had you a little spill."

"We turned over twice!" said the grandmother.

"Oncet," he corrected. "We seen it happen. Try their car and see will it run, Hiram," he said quietly to the boy with the gray hat.

"What you got that gun for?" John Wesley asked. "Whatcha gonna do with that gun?"

"Lady," the man said to the children's mother, "would you mind calling them children to sit down by you? Children make me nervous. I want all you all to sit down right together there where you're at."

"What are you telling US what to do for?" June Star asked.

Behind them the line of woods gaped like a dark open mouth. "Come here," said their mother.

"Look here now," Bailey began suddenly, "we're in a predicament! We're in . . ."

The grandmother shrieked. She scrambled to her feet and stood staring. "You're The Misfit!" she said. "I recognized you at once!"

"Yes'm," the man said, smiling slightly as if he were pleased in spite of himself to be known, "but it would have been better for all of you, lady, if you hadn't of reckernized me."

Bailey turned his head sharply and said something to his mother that shocked even the children. The old lady began to cry and The Misfit reddened.

"Lady," he said, "don't you get upset. Sometimes a man says things he don't mean. I don't reckon he meant to talk to you thataway."

"You wouldn't shoot a lady, would you?" the grandmother said and removed a clean handkerchief from her cuff and began to slap at her eyes with it.

The Misfit pointed the toe of his shoe into the ground and made a little hole and then covered it up again. "I would hate to have to," he said.

"Listen," the grandmother almost screamed, "I know you're a good man. You don't look a bit like you have common blood. I know you must come from nice people!"

"Yes mam," he said, "finest people in the world." When he smiled he showed a row of strong white teeth. "God never made a finer woman than my mother and my daddy's heart was pure gold," he said. The boy with the red sweat shirt had come around behind them and was standing with his gun at his hip. The Misfit squatted down on the ground. "Watch them children, Bobby Lee," he said. "You know they make me nervous." He looked at the six of them huddled together in front of him and he seemed to be embarrassed as if he couldn't think of anything to say. "Ain't a cloud in the sky," he remarked, looking up at it. "Don't see no sun but don't see no cloud neither."

"Yes, it's a beautiful day," said the grandmother. "Listen," she said, "you shouldn't call yourself The Misfit because I know you're a good man at heart. I can just look at you and tell."

"Hush!" Bailey yelled. "Hush! Everybody shut up and let me handle this!" He was squatting in the position of a runner about to sprint forward but he didn't move.

"I pre-chate that, lady," The Misfit said and drew a little circle in the ground with the butt of his gun.

"It'll take a half a hour to fix this here car," Hiram called, looking over the raised hood of it.

"Well, first you and Bobby Lee get him and that little boy to step over yonder with you," The Misfit said, pointing to Bailey and John Wesley. "The boys want to ast you something," he said to Bailey. "Would you mind stepping back in them woods there with them?"

"Listen," Bailey began, "we're in a terrible predicament! Nobody realizes what this is," and his voice cracked. His eyes were as blue and intense as the parrots in his shirt and he remained perfectly still.

The grandmother reached up to adjust her hat brim as if she were going to the woods with him but it came off in her hand. She stood staring at it and after a second she let it fall on the ground. Hiram pulled Bailey up by the arm as if he were assisting an old man. John Wesley caught hold of his father's hand and Bobby Lee followed. They went off toward the woods and just as they reached the dark edge, Bailey turned and supporting himself against a gray naked pine trunk, he shouted, "I'll be back in a minute, Mamma, wait on me!"

"Come back this instant!" his mother shrilled but they all disappeared into the woods.

"Bailey Boy!" the grandmother called in a tragic voice but she found she was looking at The Misfit squatting on the ground in front of her. "I just know you're a good man," she said desperately. "You're not a bit common!"

"Nome, I ain't a good man," The Misfit said after a second as if he had considered her statement carefully, "but I ain't the worst in the world neither. My daddy said I was a different breed of dog from my brothers and sisters. 'You know,' Daddy said, 'it's some that can live their whole life out without asking about it and it's others has to know why it is, and this boy is one of the latters. He's going to be into everything!'" He put on his black hat and looked up suddenly and then away deep into the woods as if he were embarrassed again. "I'm sorry I don't have on a shirt before you ladies," he said, hunching his shoulders slightly. "We buried our clothes that we had on when we escaped and we're just making do until we can get better. We borrowed these from some folks we met," he explained.

"That's perfectly all right," the grandmother said. "Maybe Bailey has an extra shirt in his suitcase."

"I'll look and see terrectly," The Misfit said.

"Where are they taking him?" the children's mother screamed.

"Daddy was a card himself," The Misfit said. "You couldn't put anything over on him. He never got in trouble with the Authorities though. Just had the knack of handling them."

"You could be honest too if you'd only try," said the grandmother. "Think how wonderful it would be to settle down and live a comfortable life and not have to think about somebody chasing you all the time."

The Misfit kept scratching in the ground with the butt of his gun as if he were thinking about it. "Yes'm, somebody is always after you," he murmured.

The grandmother noticed how thin his shoulder blades were just behind his hat because she was standing up looking down on him. "Do you every pray?" she asked.

He shook his head. All she saw was the black hat wiggle between his shoulder blades. "Nome," he said.

There was a pistol shot from the woods, followed closely by another. Then silence. The old lady's head jerked around. She could hear the wind move through the tree tops like a long satisfied insuck of breath. "Bailey Boy!" she called.

"I was a gospel singer for a while," The Misfit said. "I been most everything. Been in the arm service, both land and sea, at home and abroad, been twict married, been an undertaker, been with the railroads, plowed Mother Earth, been in a tornado, seen a man burnt alive oncet," and he looked up at the children's mother and the little girl who were sitting close together, their faces white and their eyes glassy; "I even seen a woman flogged," he said.

"Pray, pray," the grandmother began, "pray, pray . . ."

"I never was a bad boy that I remember of," The Misfit said in an almost dreamy voice, "but somewheres along the line I done something wrong and got sent to the penitentiary. I was buried alive," and he looked up and held her attention to him by a steady stare.

"That's when you should have started to pray," she said. "What did you do to get sent to the penitentiary that first time?"

"Turn to the right, it was a wall," The Misfit said, looking up again at the cloudless sky. "Turn to the left, it was a wall. Look up it was a ceiling, look down it was a floor. I forget what I done, lady. I set there and set there, trying to remember what it was I done and I ain't recalled it to this day. Oncet in a while, I would think it was coming to me, but it never come."

"Maybe they put you in by mistake," the old lady said vaguely.

"Nome," he said. "It wasn't no mistake. They had the papers on me."

"You must have stolen something," she said.

The Misfit sneered slightly. "Nobody had nothing I wanted," he said. "It was a head-doctor at the penitentiary said what I had done was kill my daddy but I known that for a lie. My daddy died in nineteen ought nineteen of the epidemic flu and I never had a thing to do with it. He was buried in the Mount Hopewell Baptist churchyard and you can go there and see for yourself."

"If you would pray," the old lady said, "Jesus would help you."

"That's right," The Misfit said.

"Well then, why don't you pray?" she asked trembling with delight suddenly.

"I don't want no hep," he said. "I'm doing all right by myself."

Bobby Lee and Hiram came ambling back from the woods. Bobby Lee was dragging a yellow shirt with bright blue parrots in it.

"Thow me that shirt, Bobby Lee," The Misfit said. The shirt came flying at him and landed on his shoulder and he put it on. The grandmother couldn't name what the shirt reminded her of. "No, lady," The Misfit said while he was buttoning it up, "I found out the crime don't matter. You can do one thing or you can do another, kill a man or take a tire off his car, because sooner or later you're going to forget what it was you done and just be punished for it."

The children's mother had begun to make heaving noises as if she couldn't get her breath. "Lady," he asked, "would you and that little girl like to step off yonder with Bobby Lee and Hiram and join your husband?"

"Yes, thank you," the mother said faintly. Her left arm dangled helplessly and she was holding the baby, who had gone to sleep, in the other. "Hep that lady up, Hiram," The Misfit said as she struggled to climb out of the ditch, "and Bobby Lee, you hold onto that little girl's hand."

"I don't want to hold hands with him," June Star said. "He reminds me of a pig."

The fat boy blushed and laughed and caught her by the arm and pulled her off into the woods after Hiram and her mother.

Alone with The Misfit, the grandmother found that she had lost her voice. There was not a cloud in the sky nor any sun. There was nothing around her but woods. She wanted to tell him that he must pray. She opened and closed her mouth several times before anything came out. Finally she found herself saying, "Jesus. Jesus," meaning, Jesus will help you, but the way she was saying it, it sounded as if she might be cursing.

"Yes'm, The Misfit said as if he agreed. "Jesus thown everything off balance. It was the same case with Him as with me except He hadn't committed any crime and they could prove I had committed one because they had the papers on me. Of course," he said, "they never shown me my papers. That's why I sign myself now. I said long ago, you get you a signature and sign everything you do and keep a copy of it. Then you'll know what you done and you can hold up the crime to the punishment and see do they match and in the end you'll have something to prove you ain't been treated right. I call myself The Misfit," he said, "because I can't make what all I done wrong fit what all I gone through in punishment."

There was a piercing scream from the woods, followed closely by a pistol report. "Does it seem right to you, lady, that one is punished a heap and another ain't punished at all?"

"Jesus!" the old lady cried. "You've got good blood! I know you wouldn't shoot a lady! I know you come from nice people! Pray! Jesus, you ought not to shoot a lady. I'll give you all the money I've got!"

"Lady," The Misfit said, looking beyond her far into the woods, "there never was a body that give the undertaker a tip."

There were two more pistol reports and the grandmother raised her head like a parched old turkey hen crying for water and called, "Bailey Boy, Bailey Boy!" as if her heart would break.

"Jesus was the only One that ever raised the dead," The Misfit continued, "and He shouldn't have done it. He thown everything off balance. If He did what He said, then it's nothing for you to do but thow away everything and follow Him, and if He didn't, then it's nothing for you to do but enjoy the few minutes you got left the best way you can—by killing somebody or burning down his house or doing some other meanness to him. No pleasure but meanness," he said and his voice had become almost a snarl.

"Maybe He didn't raise the dead," the old lady mumbled, not knowing what she was saying and feeling so dizzy that she sank down in the ditch with her legs twisted under her.

"I wasn't there so I can't say He didn't," The Misfit said. "I wisht I had of been there," he said, hitting the ground with his fist. "It ain't right I wasn't there because if I had of been there I would of known. Listen lady," he said in a high voice, "if I had of been there I would of known and I wouldn't be like I am now." His voice seemed about to crack and the grandmother's head cleared for an instant. She saw the man's face twisted close to her own as if he were going to cry and she murmured, "Why you're one of my babies. You're one of my own children!" She reached out and touched him on the shoulder. The Misfit sprang back as if a snake had bitten him and shot her three times through the chest. Then he put his gun down on the ground and took off his glasses and began to clean them.

Hiram and Bobby Lee returned from the woods and stood over the ditch, looking down at the grandmother who half sat and half lay in a puddle of blood with her legs crossed under her like a child's and her face smiling up at the cloudless sky.

Without his glasses, The Misfit's eyes were red-rimmed and pale and defenseless-looking. "Take her off and thow her where you thown the others," he said, picking up the cat that was rubbing itself against his leg.

"She was a talker, wasn't she?" Bobby Lee said, sliding down the ditch with a yodel.

"She would of been a good woman," The Misfit said, "if it had been somebody there to shoot her every minute of her life."

"Some fun!" Bobby Lee said.

"Shut up, Bobby Lee," The Misfit said. "It's no real pleasure in life."

Background to the Story

On Her Own Work

A Reasonable Use of the Unreasonable

Last fall* I received a letter from a student who said she would be "graciously appreciative" if I would tell her "just what enlightenment" I expected her to get from each of my stories. I suspect she had a paper to write. I wrote her back to forget about the enlightenment and just try to enjoy them. I knew that was the most unsatisfactory answer I could have given because, of course, she didn't want to enjoy them, she just wanted to figure them out.

In most English classes the short story has become a kind of literary specimen to be dissected. Every time a story of mine appears in a Freshman anthology, I have a vision of it, with its little organs laid open, like a frog in a bottle.

I realize that a certain amount of this what-is-the-significance has to go on, but I think something has gone wrong in the process when, for so many students, the story becomes simply a problem to be solved, something which you evaporate to get Instant Enlightenment.

A story really isn't any good unless it successfully resists paraphrase, unless it hangs on and expands in the mind.

From *Mystery and Manners,* ed. Sally and Robert Fitzgerald (New York: Farrar, Straus and Giroux, 1969), 107–114.

*I.e., in 1962. These remarks were made by Flannery O'Connor at Hollins College, Virginia, to introduce a reading of her story, "A Good Man Is Hard to Find," on October 14, 1963.

Properly, you analyze to enjoy, but it's equally true that to analyze with any discrimination, you have to have enjoyed already, and I think that the best reason to hear a story read is that it should stimulate that primary enjoyment.

I don't have any pretensions to being an Aeschylus or Sophocles and providing you in this story with a cathartic experience out of your mythic background, though this story I'm going to read certainly calls up a good deal of the South's mythic background, and it should elicit from you a degree of pity and terror, even though its way of being serious is a comic one. I do think, though, that like the Greeks, you should know what is going to happen in this story so that any element of suspense in it will be transferred from its surface to its interior.

I would be most happy if you had already read it, happier still if you knew it well, but since experience has taught me to keep my expectations along these lines modest, I'll tell you that this is the story of a family of six which, on its way driving to Florida, gets wiped out by an escaped convict who calls himself the Misfit. The family is made up of the Grandmother and her son, Bailey, and his children, John Wesley and June Star and the baby, and there is also the cat and the children's mother. The cat is named Pitty Sing, and the Grandmother is taking him with them, hidden in a basket.

Now I think it behooves me to try to establish with you the basis on which reason operates in this story. Much of my fiction takes its character from a reasonable use of the unreasonable, though the reasonableness of my use of it may not always be apparent. The assumptions that underlie this use of it, however, are those of the central Christian mysteries. These are assumptions to which a large part of the modern audience takes exception. About this I can only say that there are perhaps other ways than my own in which this story could be read, but none other by which it could have been written.

Belief, in my own case anyway, is the engine that makes perception operate.

The heroine of this story, the Grandmother, is in the most significant position life offers the Christian. She is facing death. And to all appearances she, like the rest of us, is not too well prepared for it. She would like to see the event postponed. Indefinitely.

I've talked to a number of teachers who use this story in class and who tell their students that the Grandmother is evil, that in fact, she's a witch, even down to the cat. One of these teachers told me that his students, and particularly his Southern students, resisted this interpretation with a certain bemused vigor, and he didn't understand why. I had to tell him that they resisted it because they all had grandmothers or great-aunts just like her at home, and they knew, from personal experience, that the old lady lacked comprehension, but that she had a good heart. The Southerner is usually tolerant of those weaknesses that proceed from innocence, and he knows that a taste for self-preservation can be readily combined with the missionary spirit.

The same teacher was telling his students that morally the Misfit was several cuts above the Grandmother. He had a really sentimental attachment to the Misfit. But then a prophet gone wrong is almost always more interesting than your grandmother, and you have to let people take their pleasures where they find them.

It is true that the old lady is a hypocritical old soul; her wits are no match for the Misfit's, nor is her capacity for grace equal to his; yet I think the unprejudiced reader will feel that the Grandmother has a special kind of triumph in this story which instinctively we do not allow to someone altogether bad.

I often ask myself what makes a story work, and what makes it hold up as a story, and I have decided that it is probably some action, some gesture of a character that is unlike any other in the story, one which indicates where the real heart of the story lies. This would have to be an action or a gesture which was both totally right and totally unexpected; it would have to be one that was both in character and beyond character; it would have to suggest both the world and eternity. The action or gesture I'm talking about would have to be on the anagogical level, that is, the level which has to do with the Divine life and our participation in it. It would be a gesture that transcended any neat allegory that might have been intended or any pat moral categories a reader could make. It would be a gesture which somehow made contact with mystery.

There is a point in this story where such a gesture occurs. The Grandmother is at last alone, facing the Misfit. Her head clears for an instant and she realizes, even in her limited way, that she is responsible for the man before her and joined to him by ties of kinship which have their roots deep in the mystery she has been merely prattling about so far. And at this point, she does the right thing, she makes the right gesture.

I find that students are often puzzled by what she says and does here, but I think myself that if I took out this gesture and what she says with it, I would have no story. What was left would not be worth your attention. Our age not only does not have a very sharp eye for the almost imperceptible intrusions of grace, it no longer has much feeling for the nature of the violences which precede and follow them. The devil's greatest wile, Baudelaire has said, is to convince us that he does not exist.

I suppose the reasons for the use of so much violence in modern fiction will differ with each writer who uses it, but in my own stories I have found that violence is strangely capable of returning my characters to reality and preparing them to accept their moment of grace. Their heads are so hard that almost nothing else will do the work. This idea, that reality is something to which we must be returned at considerable cost, is one which is seldom understood by the casual reader, but it is one which is implicit in the Christian view of the world.

I don't want to equate the Misfit with the devil. I prefer to think that, however unlikely this may seem, the old lady's gesture, like the mustard-seed, will grow to be a great crow-filled tree in the Misfit's heart, and will be enough of a pain to him there to turn him into the prophet he was meant to become.[1] But that's another story.

This story has been called grotesque, but I prefer to call it literal. A good story is literal in the same sense that a child's drawing is literal. When a child draws, he doesn't intend to distort but to set down exactly what he sees, and as his gaze is direct, he sees the lines that create motion. Now the lines of motion that interest the writer are usually invisible. They are lines of spiritual motion. And in this story you should be on the lookout for such things as the action of grace in the Grandmother's soul, and not for the dead bodies.

We hear many complaints about the prevalence of violence in modern fiction, and it is always assumed that this violence is a bad thing and meant to be an end in itself. With the serious writer, violence is never an end in itself. It is the extreme situation that best reveals what we are essentially, and I believe these are times when writers are more interested in what we are essentially than in the tenor of our daily lives. Violence is a force which can be used for good or evil, and among other things taken by it is the kingdom of heaven. But regardless of what can be taken by it, the man in the violent situation reveals those qualities least dispensable in his personality, those qualities which are all he will have to take into eternity with him; and since the characters in this story are all on the verge of eternity, it is appropriate to think of what they take with them. In any case, I hope that if you consider these points in connection with the story, you will come to see it as something more than an account of a family murdered on the way to Florida.

Notes

1. See Matthew 13:31–32; Mark 4:31–32; Luke 13:19 [Ed.'s note].

Letters

To John Hawkes

14 April 60

. . . It's interesting to me that your students naturally work their way to the idea that the Grandmother in "A Good Man" is not pure evil and may be a medium for Grace. If they were Southern students I would say this was because they all had grandmothers like her at home. These old ladies exactly reflect the banalities of the society and the effect is of the comical rather than the seriously evil. But Andrew [Lytle] insists that she is a witch, even down to the cat. These children, yr. students, know their grandmothers aren't witches.

Perhaps it is a difference in theology, or rather the difference that ingrained theology makes in the sensibility. Grace, to the Catholic way of thinking, can and does use as its medium the imperfect, purely human, and even hypocritical. Cutting yourself off from Grace is a very decided matter, requiring a real choice, act of will, and affecting the very ground of the soul. The Misfit is touched by the Grace that comes through the old lady when she recognizes him as her child, as she has been touched by the Grace that comes through him in his particular suffering. His shooting her is a recoil, a horror at her humanness, but after he has done it and cleaned his glasses, the Grace has worked in him and he pronounces his judgment: she would have been a good woman if *he* had been there every moment of her life. True enough. In the Protestant view, I think Grace and nature don't have much to do with

---

From *The Habit of Being: Letters of Flannery O'Connor*, ed. Sally Fitzgerald (New York: Farrar, Straus and Giroux, 1979), 389–390, 436–437.

each other. The old lady, because of her hypocrisy and humanness and banality couldn't be a medium for Grace. In the sense that I see things the other way, I'm a Catholic writer. . . .

A professor of English had sent Flannery the following letter: "I am writing as spokesman for three members of our department and some ninety university students in three classes for a week have been discussing your story 'A Good Man Is Hard to Find.' We have debated at length several possible interpretations, none of which fully satisfies us. In general we believe that the appearance of the Misfit is not 'real' in the same sense that the incidents of the first half of the story are real. Bailey, we believe, imagines the appearance of the Misfit, whose activities have been called to his attention on the night before the trip and again during the stopover at the roadside restaurant. Bailey, we further believe, identifies himself with the Misfit and so plays two roles in the imaginary last half of the story. But we cannot, after great effort, determine the point at which reality fades into illusion or reverie. Does the accident literally occur, or is it a part of Bailey's dream? Please believe me when I say we are not seeking an easy way out of our difficulty. We admire your story and have examined it with great care, but we are convinced that we are missing something important which you intended for us to grasp. We will all be very grateful if you comment on the interpretation which I have outlined above and if you will give us further comments about your intention in writing 'A Good Man Is Hard to Find.'"

She replied:

To a Professor of English

28 March 61

The interpretation of your ninety students and three teachers is fantastic and about as far from my intentions as it could get to be. If it were long a legitimate interpretation, the story would be little more than a trick and its interest would be simply for abnormal psychology. I am not interested in abnormal psychology.

There is a change of tension from the first part of the story to the second where the Misfit enters, but this is no lessening of reality. This story is, of course, not meant to be realistic in the sense that it portrays the everyday doings of people in Georgia. It is stylized and its conventions are comic even though its meaning is serious.

Bailey's only importance is as the Grandmother's boy and the driver of the car. It is the Grandmother who first there recognizes the Misfit and who is most concerned with him throughout. The story is a duel of sorts between the Grandmother and her superficial beliefs and the Misfit's more profoundly felt involvement with Christ's action which set the world off balance for him.

The meaning of a story should go on expanding for the reader the more he thinks about it, but meaning cannot be captured in an interpretation. If teachers are in the habit of approaching a story as if it were a research problem for which any answer is believable so long as it is not obvious, then I think students will never learn to enjoy fiction. Too much interpretation is certainly worse than too little, and where feeling for a story is absent, theory will not supply it.

My tone is not meant to be obnoxious. I am in a state of shock.

Critical Essays

J. O. TATE

A Good Source Is Not So Hard to Find

The mounting evidence of O'Connor's use of items from the Milledgeville and Atlanta newspapers will interest those who realize that these sources, in and of themselves, have nothing to do with the Gothic, the grotesque, the American Romance tradition, Southwestern humor, Southern literature, adolesescent aggression, the New Hermeneutics, the anxiety of influence, structuralism, pentecostal Gnosticism, medieval theology, Christian humanism, existentialism, or the Roman Catholic Church.

I. On "The Misfit" as Name and Word

The text of an Atlanta *Constitution* article of November 6, 1952, p. 29, identifies for us the source of a celebrated sobriquet. This newspaper reference was reprinted in *The Flannery O'Connor Bulletin,* Volume III, Autumn 1974. The headline says enough: "'The Misfit' Robs Office, Escapes With $150." Flannery O'Connor took a forgotten criminal's alias and used it for larger purposes: *her* Misfit was out of place in a grander way than the original. But we should not forget O'Connor's credentials as "a literalist of the imagination." There is always "a little lower layer." She meant to mock pop psychology by exploiting the original Misfit's exploitation of a socio-psychological "excuse" for aberrant behavior. But even a little lower:

From *The Flannery O'Connor Bulletin* 9 (1980): 98–102.

the original meaning of the word "misfit" has to do with clothing. We should not fail, therefore, to note that The Misfit's "borrowed" blue jeans are too tight. He leaves the story, of course, wearing Bailey's shirt.

II. On the Identity and Destiny of the Original Misfit

By November 15, 1952, The Misfit had been apprehended; he had also advanced himself to page three of The Atlanta *Journal*. The Misfit was a twenty-five-year old named James C. Yancey. He "was found to be of unsound mind" and committed to the state mental hospital at—Milledgeville. Where else?

III. On The Misfit's Notoriety, Peregrinations, Good Manners, Eye-glasses, Companions, and Mental Hygiene

The original Misfit was, as criminals go, small potatoes. He was an unambitious thief, no more. O'Connor took nothing from him but his imposing signature. But it just so happens that there was another well-publicized criminal aloose in Tennessee and Georgia just before the time that O'Connor appropriated the Misfit's name. This other hold-up artist had four important qualities in common with *her* Misfit. First, he inspired a certain amount of terror through several states. Second, he had, or claimed to have, a certain *politesse*. Third, he wore spectacles. Fourth, he had two accomplices, in more than one account.

James Francis ("Three-Gun") Hill, the sinister celebrity of the front pages, much more closely resembles the object of the grandmother's warnings than the original Misfit. Various articles tell of "a fantastic record of 26 kidnappings in four states, as many robberies, 10 car thefts, and a climactic freeing of four Florida convicts from a prison gang—all in two kaleidoscopic weeks." He had advanced "from an obscure hoodlum to top billing as a public enemy" (The Atlanta *Constitution,* November 1, p. 1). Such headlines as the grandmother had in mind screamed of Hill (though not in the sports section that Bailey was reading): "Maniac's Gang Terrorizes Hills" (*Constitution,* October 24, p. 2, from Sparta, Tenn.); "Search for Kidnap-Robbery Trio Centers in Atlanta and Vicinity" (October 25, p. 1, from Atlanta); "Chattanooga Is Focal Point for Manhunt" (October 27, p. 26); "2nd of Terror Gang Seized In Florida/Pal Said Still In Atlanta Area" (October 29, p. 32); "Self-Styled 3-Gun Maniac Frees 4 Road Gang Convicts at Gunpoint" (October 31, p. 1, from Bartow, Florida). It is quite clear that O'Connor, imagining through the grandmother's point of view, was, like the newspapers, assuming an Atlanta locale and orientation. The southward trip was in the same direction as Hill's last run.

The article of October 24 gives us a bit of color: "A fantastic band of highwaymen, led by a self-styled 'maniac' who laughed weirdly while he looted his victims, spread terror through the Cumberland hills today. . . . [The leader] boasted that he had escaped from the Utah State Prison and 'killed two people' . . . 'They call me a three-gun maniac, and brother, they got the picture straight,' the head bandit was quoted by victims." The October 31 article hints at the rustic setting of O'Connor's story: "The escapers and Hill . . . drove up a dead-end road and abandoned the car. They fled into thick woods on foot. . . ."

The *Constitution* of November 1 speaks of Hill on the front page as "the bespectacled, shrunken-cheeked highwayman." A later article gives us, as it gave O'Connor, a clue to her Misfit's respectful modes of address ("Good afternoon . . . I pre-chate that, lady . . . Nome . . . I'm sorry I don't have on a shirt before you ladies . . . Yes'm . . ."): We read of the trial of "Accused kidnapper, James Francis (Three-Gun) Hill, who says he's a 'gentleman-bandit' because 'I didn't cuss in front of ladies. . . .'" This Associated Press wire story from Chattanooga was on page 26 of the November 13 Atlanta *Journal.*

The *Constitution* of the same date says "Hearing Delayed for 'Maniac' Hill and 2 Cronies," and goes on to mention "James Francis Hill, self-styled 'three-gun maniac.'" We may observe that both Yancey and Hill were referred to in the newspapers as "self-styled," an arresting phrase perhaps to an author attuned to extravagances of self. I think we may also recognize here the genesis of Hiram and Bobby Lee.

The result of Hill's plea of guilty was perhaps not as forthright as his intention: "'Maniac Hill Is Adjudged Incompetent" (*Constitution,* November 18). Like Yancey, The Misfit, Hill was sent to a mental institution—in Tennessee, this time. (His cronies were sentenced to jail.) The diagnosis of both Yancey and Hill as mentally ill may have suggested O'Connor's Misfit's experiences with the "head-doctor."

IV. On The Misfit, Memory, and Guilt

The fictional Misfit was not easily freudened: he knew perfectly well that he had not killed his daddy. Yet he insisted there was no balance between guilt and punishment—if memory served.

The issues of accuracy of memory, consciousness of guilt, and conscience were also raised in an odd "human-interest" story that was published in those same days when O'Connor was gathering so much material from the newspapers. The Misfit's claim that he was punished for crimes he did not remember may have been inspired by this account of a man who was *not* punished for a crime he *did* remember—but remembered wrongly.

The *Journal* of November 5, 1952 carried the article, written from Brookhaven, New York, on page 12: "'Murder' Didn't Happen, House Painter Free." Louis Roberts had shot a policeman in 1928; he assumed he had killed him. Over twenty years later, his conscience finally forced him to confess. When his tale was investigated, it was discovered that the policeman had survived after all. There was no prosecution for, as an authority was quoted as saying, "His conscience has punished him enough."

HALLMAN B. BRYANT

Reading the Map in "A Good Man Is Hard to Find"

Flannery O'Connor, remarking on her most famous short story, "A Good Man Is Hard to Find," issues several caveats to critics. She allows that "a certain amount of what is the significance of this" kind of investigation has to go on in teaching and in literary analysis, but she cautions against reducing a story to "a problem to be solved" so that it becomes "something which you evaporate to get Instant Enlightenment."

Without evaporating too much I will try to shed light on the significance of some small details in "A Good Man Is Hard to Find." Although I do not think an analysis of O'Connor's use of place names in the story will create instant enlightenment, I believe that the towns alluded to along the route which the family travels were chosen for two reasons: first, and most obviously, to foreshadow; and second, to augment the theme of the story. Furthermore, because the numerous places mentioned in the story can actually be found on the map, with only one important exception, it is thus possible to estimate within a few miles the physical distance that the family travels.

The first thing one notices about "A Good Man Is Hard to Find" is that it is set in a real place—in the state of Georgia. The opening scene describes an Atlanta family quarreling about their vacation plans. The grandmother is opposed to

From *Studies in Short Fiction* 18 (1981): 301–307.

going to Florida ostensibly because a convict "that calls himself The Misfit is aloose from the Federal pen and headed toward Florida." (Apparently the Federal penitentiary from which the Misfit has escaped is the one in Atlanta, although it is not specified in the story.) Regardless of the threat posed by The Misfit, the family heads south for Florida instead of east Tennessee where the grandmother had tried to persuade them to take her. We are told that the family left Atlanta at 8:35 in the morning with the mileage on the car at 55,890, a fact recorded by the grandmother because she "thought it would be interesting to say how many miles they had been when they got back." From this point on one can literally follow the journey of the family with a road map and take the mileage they put on their car before the wreck and the subsequent meeting with The Misfit and his henchmen.

One odd fact about their route emerges immediately to anyone familiar with Atlanta and its environs. Although the family lives in Atlanta and is headed south, we are told that they pass Stone Mountain along the way. This natural phenomenon and tourist attraction is about fifteen or sixteen miles from Atlanta on the northeast side of the city. At the time the story was written, one had to follow U.S. 78 North to get to Stone Mountain, a highly unlikely road to take out of Atlanta if one is going to Florida.[1]

Although one of the children urges his father to "go through Georgia fast so we won't have to look at it much," there nevertheless are some interesting details of scenery along the roadside, and the grandmother tells us about many of the things they pass by. She notices "a cute little pickaninny" standing in the door of a shanty that she fancies would make a nice study for a sentimental painting, but the same subject disgusts her granddaughter June Star, who comments acidly, "He didn't have any britches on." More significantly, the grandmother points out a graveyard with five or six graves fenced off in the middle of a large cotton field, which is a rather obvious foreshadowing of the fate that will befall the family.

When the grandmother can no longer hold the children's attention with roadside attractions, she tells them a story of one of her girlhood suitors, Mr. Edgar Atkins Teagarden, who was from Jasper, Georgia, a small north Georgia town located in Pickens County and approximately fifty or sixty miles from the Tennessee state line. Although we are not told just where the grandmother is from, only that she has "connections in east Tennessee," it seems that to be consistent with her tale of Mr. Teagarden's courtship, she would have to have lived somewhere near Jasper, since he drove to her house by buggy every Saturday and gave her a watermelon monogrammed with his initials, E. A. T.

The family's journey is interrupted by a stop for a lunch of barbecued sandwiches at a café called The Tower which is located in "a clearing outside of Timothy." For comic effect this is one of the great scenes in all of Flannery O'Connor's fiction; yet, here one cannot plot the location of the place on the map for there is no town of Timothy in Georgia. (If there is, it is such a small community it is not listed in the state atlas.) Since the other references to places in the story are to actual localities in the state, why does she create a fictitious name at this point? My theory is that in this scene, which has strong moral intention, O'Connor selected the name Timothy for the ironic effect it would produce. The allusion here is not geographical but Biblical, and the Timothy alluded to is almost certainly the book in the New Testament which bears the same name. Usually referred to as the Pastoral Letters, this gospel purports to be letters from Paul addressed to his disciples and through them to the Christian community at large. More than any other writing in the New Testament, the letters to Timothy are concerned with Christian orthodoxy. In this gospel Paul deals essentially with three topics: the opposition of false doctrine; the organization of the church and establishment of ecclesiastical regulations; and exhortations which indicate how to be a good citizen and Christian.

It seems to me that the concerns expressed by Paul in his letter to Timothy are very germane to the concerns expressed by Flannery O'Connor in "A Good Man Is Hard to Find," especially the concern with heretics and the advice on how to be a good Christian. One has only to set the family of six from Atlanta and Red Sammy and his wife (as well as The Misfit)—all of whom Flannery O'Connor considers heretics—against certain passages from Timothy to see that O'Connor's allusion ironically tells us just where these modern-day people are in error. For example, these verses seem to apply especially to Bailey. "He [the husband] must manage his own family well and see that his children obey him with proper respect" (I Tim. 3:4–5).

Also the author of the epistle commands good Christians to keep the faith and avoid "vain discussions" and concern with trivial matters and endless wrangling about genealogies (I Tim. 6:3–10). Further, he admonishes women "to dress modestly, with decency and propriety" and "to learn in quietness and full submission . . . and be silent" (I Tim. 2:9–12). This instruction seems to bear most directly on the grandmother, who is vain about her Old South heritage and certainly conscious of her social standing and what is required to be a lady. This is best brought out in her selection of attire for the trip. She is turned out in white gloves, black purse, a navy blue straw sailor hat with white violets on the brim, a navy blue polka dot dress with collar and cuffs of white organdy trimmed with lace, and on her neck she has pinned a purple spray of cloth violets containing a sachet. Her costume has been prepared so that, in the event of an accident, "anyone seeing her dead on the highway would know at once that she was a lady."

The grandmother's superficial conception of values is ironically underscored in the vain discussions with her grandchildren about what kind of conduct was once expected from children and her trivial remarks about plantation days and old suitors. Nowhere are her ideas more tellingly satirized than in her conversation with Red Sammy in the café where both complain of misplaced trust in their fellow man, which the grandmother sees as an indication of the general lack of manners in the modern world. She tells Red Sammy, "People are certainly not nice like they used to be." Of course, both Red Sammy and the grandmother are conceited enough to think that they are just as good as they ought to be. When Red Sammy complains of a recent theft of some gasoline by men driving a Chrysler and asks in a puzzled way why he had trusted them, he is quickly told by the grandmother that it was "because you're a good man," to which he candidly assents, "Yes'm, I suppose so."

The grandmother's inability to "learn in quietness" is tragically the cause of the deaths of the entire family. Shortly after Bailey overturns the car in a ditch, they are approached by a bespectacled man who the grandmother feels is "someone she knew" and soon she recognizes the stranger as The Misfit whose picture she has seen, and she blurts out this fact, saying, "You're The Misfit . . . I recognized you at once," to which he replies, "but it would have been better for all of you, lady, if you hadn't of reckernized me."

It is generally agreed that in the traumatic moments that follow in which the grandmother witnesses the deaths of her family and anticipates her own she does learn a lesson she has not heeded previously during her life. This lesson is the central message which Paul attempts to convey to Christians through Timothy and that is, "There is one God and one mediator between God and men, the Lord Jesus Christ, who gave himself to save mankind" (I Tim. 2:5). The evidence for assuming that she has come to a belated awareness that her faith has been misplaced in the pursuit of social graces and a concern with manners is limited to The Misfit's remark, "She would have been a good woman . . . if it had been somebody there to shoot her every minute of her life." Furthermore, in death she appears like a child, and her face is "smiling up at the cloudless sky," suggesting that she has found grace at last.

Another passage from Timothy seems especially applicable at this point: "The Spirit clearly says that in later times some will abandon the faith and follow deceiving spirits and things taught by demons. Such teachings come through hypocritical liars, whose consciences have been seared as with hot iron" (I Tim. 4:1–12). Although the whole cast of characters in the story has abandoned the faith and followed the wrong paths, the indictment of these lines would apply most forcibly to The Misfit who wears glasses and has a scholarly look. He has indeed been taught by demons, and from the Christian point of view that O'Connor takes in "A Good Man Is Hard to Find" he is a hypocritical liar who has no faith in a moral purpose in the universe and teaches that "it's nothing for you to do but enjoy the few minutes you got left the best way you can—by killing somebody or burning down his house or doing some other meanness to him." Thus, according to the ethics of this teacher, goodness is a matter of sadistic gratification. "No pleasure but meanness," he says, indicating how completely his conscience has been seared and his vision warped by his hedonistic atheism.

The numerous ways in which the content of this book of the New Testament dovetails with the characters and the theme of "A Good Man Is Hard to Find" could not be a complete accident. It cannot be demonstrated that Flannery O'Connor conceived of the moral of her story in terms of this specific book, but she made no bones about the fact that she wrote "from the standpoint of Christian orthodoxy;"[2] and there is no doubt that Paul wrote from a similar standpoint, and his letter to Timothy has the same hortatory, moralizing tone that we find just below the surface in "A Good Man Is Hard to Find." Thus, it seems likely that she put the town of Timothy on the map because she wanted the reader to pick up the allusion and perhaps refresh himself on the contents of the New Testament, but more probably she saw the parallel between her modern-day characters who have left the main road of Christian faith and Paul's warning to the church when he feared it was in danger off into the byways of heresy.

Just as the name of the town where the family stops for lunch is carefully chosen, so is the name of Red Sammy's café. In Christian iconography towers are ambivalent symbols, that is, they speak *in bono* or *in malo,* to use the vocabulary of medieval exegetes, and can represent either good or evil qualities. For example, the Tower of Babel is symbolic of man's pride and stands for misbegotten human enterprises. The fate of the tower and its architects shows the consequences of overconfidence in the pursuit of fanciful ideas. (Interestingly enough, Nimrod, who began the construction of the tower, was also a mighty hunter, and like Red Sammy, a keeper of wild game, if Red Sammy's monkey can be called wild.)

As well as its nugatory meaning, the tower is a traditional symbol of the Virgin Mary and is a token of her purity and powers of transformation. Mary as the "refuge of sinners" according to Catholic doctrine is appropriately represented by the tower, a place associated with safety and sanctuary.

Outside of its Christian meaning the tower in arcane lore is a portent of disaster. In the sixteenth enigma of the Tarot pack of cards, catastrophe is indicated by the image of a tower struck by lightning. Whether O'Connor knew this fact about the meaning of the tower is uncertain, but she could not have been unaware of the former implications of the tower as a symbol, versed as she was in Biblical and church lore. It is appropriate that the conceited owner of this barbecue palace should have called it The Tower; it is ironic that this tower has no capacity to transform or give refuge.

Leaving Timothy and The Tower behind, both in the Biblical and geographical sense, the family resumes their trip and we are told that just beyond Toombsboro, Georgia, the grandmother awakens from a nap with the recollection, mistaken as it turns out, that there is an old plantation nearby which she had visited as a girl; she even thinks she remembers the road to take to get there and tells Bailey, "It's not far from here, I know. . . . It wouldn't take over twenty minutes." As it so happens there is a Toomsboro (spelled without the "b") on the map and it is only twenty-three miles south of Milledgeville, Flannery O'Connor's home. She surely knew the place and chose to mention it because the name has an ominous ring, and it also would have been a logical terminus for the family's trip in terms of the time and distance they have traveled since leaving Atlanta in the morning. In fact, if one follows the usual route from Atlanta to Milledgeville (Georgia Highway 212), the distance is 93 miles, and if one adds to this the 23 miles further to Toomsboro, plus the estimated 15 or so miles that the detour to the plantation takes, then it can be calculated that the family has come a total of 130 miles. Considering the conditions of Georgia roads in the late 1940s, one had to drive under 50 m.p.h. to keep from knocking the wheels out of line from the numerous potholes that Governor Talmadge's highway people never patched. Thus, if one assumes that Bailey has averaged around 45 m.p.h. and takes account of the lunch stop, they have been on the road four or five hours and their meeting with The Misfit occurs in the early afternoon of a cloudless day with the mileage on the car standing at about 56,020 on the meter. Sadly enough, the grandmother will be forever unaware of this "interesting fact," but we as readers should have a better understanding of how carefully O'Connor has used realistic detail for symbolic effects.

In the course of this story, the family's trip takes them from their complacent and smug living room to a confrontation with ultimate evil and ultimate reality as well. They are not prepared for the meeting because, like the heretics who concerned Paul in his epistle to Timothy, they have been occupied with the trivial things and involved in quarrels; and, like the builders of the Tower of Babel, they are preoccupied with vain enterprises.

Flannery O'Connor saw herself as a prophetic writer and her authorial strategy was to shock; her fiction is intended as a rebuke to rationalistic, materialistic and humanistic thought—the heresies of the twentieth century. She believed that people in the modern world were not following the true path and had to be made to see their condition for what it was—a wandering by the wayside. In "A Good Man Is Hard to Find" the family's wayward lives are given direction in their final moments, and from O'Connor's point of view they are at last on the right road.

Notes

1. The detour by Stone Mountain was probably due to O'Connor's uncertainty about its exact location; she simply found it a convenient allusion since Stone Mountain was for years Georgia's most famous tourist attraction, but perhaps there is more than meets the eye. In 1915 a project was begun by the United Daughters of the Confederacy which called for Robert E. Lee and his lieutenants to be carved in heroic scale on the vertical face of the mountain. Ironically, the artist commissioned for the job was a Yankee sculptor named Gutzon Borglum who blasted and chiseled on the mountain until 1928 when funds and patience ran out. After expenditure of hundreds of thousands of dollars in a vain effort to impose the heroes of the "Lost Cause" on the side of the mountain, the project was dropped. The scarred carvings, empty catwalks and scaffolds were reminders of a long series of errors and frustrations of the U.D.C. ladies who dreamed of keeping the past alive with a memorial that would be "the perpetuation of a vision." (See *The Story of Stone Mountain* by Willard Neal [Atlanta: Neal and Rogers, 1963], pp. 23–33). Flannery O'Connor was amused by the quixotic qualities of the U.D.C., and Stone Mountain would evoke for Georgians of

O'Connor's generation the folly of a sentimental project—a project almost as futile as the grandmother's in the story, whose fascination with past grandeur is congruent with that of the U.D.C.'s and has equally unfortunate results.

2. *The Habit of Being: Letters of Flannery O'Connor, ed.* Sally Fitzgerald (New York: Farrar, Straus and Giroux, 1979), 196.

W. S. MARKS, III

Advertisements for Grace: Flannery O'Connor's "A Good Man Is Hard to Find"

As a narrative stylist, Flannery O'Connor belongs, however peripherally, to a Pauline or Augustinian tradition extending from Langland to Bunyan and Hawthorne. Her tastes for gothicism, allegory, and regional setting derive from that special admiration for *The House of the Seven Gables* evident in so many important Southern writers from Faulkner to Truman Capote. The mingled scorn and sorrow with which Hawthorne faced the decline of New England, his ambivalent attitude towards Puritanism, and his dubious hopefulness about America's spiritual future find echoes throughout Miss O'Connor's stories of Evangelical awakening amid the scattered ashes of plantation Georgia. In "The Fiction Writer and His Country," she makes this statement about writers in the South:

> The anguish that most of us have observed for some time now has been caused not by the fact that the South is alienated from the rest of the country, but by the fact that it is not alienated enough, that every day we are getting more and more like the rest of the country, that we are being forced out, not only of our many sins, but of our few virtues.[1]

From *Studies in Short Fiction* 4 (1966): 19–27.

Further isolated from most of her contemporaries by virtue of her staunch Catholicism, Miss O'Connor reminds us less, perhaps, of Hawthorne than of Orestes Brownson, the apostate from Transcendentalism who was converted to Rome, to Calhoun, and to the notion that only a Catholic block could stem the tide of Democratic progress which was sweeping from the land all its traditional and spiritual values.

Temperamentally, Miss O'Connor displays more in common with such lay preachers of the New Left as LeRoi Jones and James Baldwin than with any specifically Southern or Catholic reaction. Similar to Baldwin's, her gripe against white liberalism grew out of a sense of estrangement from its ultimate and unannounced purpose: the homogenizing of all racial, regional, and religious cultures into one uniform and godless civilization. Her increasing frustration with this unholy prospect produced a formula: 'Were it not for the diabolic anodynes of secular liberalism man would at once recognize his hopeless depravity and degradation, repent, and be saved from the hell of this world; out and out demonism, because it openly declares man's sinful nature, must on the other hand be regarded as salutary and even admirable.' Behind this philosophy is a fascination with Dostoyevsky easily discoverable too in the Negro radicals of her generation.

Not incidentally, many of the figures in Miss O'Connor's personal pantheon have Calvinist backgrounds. It is, finally, with Evangelicalism and with the more eschatologically preoccupied varieties of religious existentialism that her work reveals its deepest affinities. Through a humorousness notably lacking in Baldwin, she speaks just as fondly of the wrath to come. "God's grace burns," she tells her readers, excusing the characteristic violence of her plots as pious metaphor. An author's consistent choice of metaphors nevertheless has inevitable implications beyond pure technique. There is, moreover, a distinction to be made between grace (which can also fall as the morning dew) and mere metaphysical evil. Miss O'Connor's further anxiousness to demonstrate the irresistibility of this grace reduces her characters to hollow recipients of divine impulse. Like rudely carved figures in some cosmic marionette show, they twitch on their wires as the indifferent spirit moves them—either to bizarre acts of criminal insanity or to equally incredible decisions for Christ. While virtue consists in conversion, sin lies in the deplorably human tendency to cut oneself loose from the puppet master, to become independently articulate. The apocalyptic terrors she visits on those who follow this atheistic course, either from bucolic ignorance or false academic sophistication, are awful to behold.

Favoring an older and more romantic mode, Flannery O'Connor rejected literary realism for much the same temperamental reasons that led her to despise other aspects of contemporary American culture. A college generation presently repudiating the liberalism of their ancestors will scarcely fail to appreciate her dogged efforts to caricaturize and deflate this public wisdom. The rare and incurable disease that crippled her and eventually took her life doubtless encouraged her to question the very basis of liberalism: the naive faith that among them democracy, free enterprise, and science hold both the explanation and permanent cure for human suffering. Because the riddle of man's incurable mortality, his subjection to physical and metaphysical torment, could not be separated from moral evil and original sin, the Freudian *Aufklärung* that had sought to evaporate these mysteries was a blasphemous lie. The mental disturbances that, along with club feet, amputated legs, myopia, and various other bodily disorders, distinguish a host of O'Connor characters, their author quaintly conceives as a species of demonic possession. Christ, who makes foolish the wisdom of her fictional world, is its only true physician. In the Raskolnikovian analysis of The Misfit, one of the more lethal and sadistic of her antiheroes: "Jesus was the only One that ever raised the dead . . . and He shouldn't have done it. He thown everything off balance. If He did what He said, then it's nothing for you to do but thow away everything and follow Him, and if He didn't, then it's nothing for you to do but enjoy the few minutes you got left the best way you can—by killing somebody or burning down his house or doing some other meanness to him. No pleasure but meanness." One of Miss O'Connor's chief delights was to parody worldly wisdom through an ironic emphasis on the clichés and advertising slogans that summarize it. Frequently stock expressions—The Life You Save May Be Your Own, A Good Man Is Hard To Find—constitute disguised advertisements for the spirit. Truth, it is thus pointed out, is only hidden from the wise. For those who will hear Him, Christ speaks even from billboards. For those who won't, Miss O'Connor reserved an audience with Death and the Devil, two of her most persuasive spokesmen.

In "A Good Man Is Hard to Find," one of the most characteristic and frequently anthologized of her pieces, these allegorical figures fool old Grandma Worldliwise with plausible Southern accents that may, however, give them away to the constant reader. Nominally set in backwoods Georgia (A "romantic precinct" on the order of Hardy's Wessex or Faulkner's Yoknapatawpha), the action of the story expands parabolically into a narrative of modern man's general sin-sickness. In bare outline, the plot concerns the tragi-comic destruction of some Florida-bound Georgians, chiefly through the senile offices of a grandmother who craftily, if unintentionally, detours her son and his family into the hands of a homicidal maniac called The Misfit. The main business of the plot, a pleasure trip to the Sunshine State, neatly epitomizes America's commercialized dream of happiness. Although each member of the family cherishes his own peculiar means of self-gratification, they are united in a common pursuit of pleasure. Enjoyment, we notice, becomes increasingly vicarious with each succeeding generation. The needs of little John Wesley and June Star are for the most part answered by Coca-Colas and, less immediately, by the promised excitement of strange new places. Mother spends her extra nickels on the juke box, which obliges her fancy with "The Tennessee Waltz"—perhaps the most popular tune ever recorded. Sadly, but necessarily, Grandmother depends on the flattering distortions of an indifferent memory. Naturally placed in a weak and unfavorable position, she is the most resourceful and least scrupulous in attaining her ends. The old woman has lived longer than her family only to develop its distinguishing trait of vain self-regard into a case of fatal hubris. The fabrication which the grandmother uses to implement her scheme of detouring Bailey Boy past the scene of badly confused girlhood memories is eagerly swallowed by John Wesley and June Star only because it serves to promote their own craving for spurious adventure.

Florida, land of the fabled fountain of youth, remains beyond the horizon, just as Grandma's romantic plantation house (which is not where she remembered it) also proves elusive. Man is the victim of irreversible time. Thus the "ACCIDENT" that prevents this arrival and is occasioned by the sudden and expressly forbidden presence of Grandma's cat, may also fall into the categories of moral or metaphysical necessity. Still the plot leans heavily and deliberately on chance, and especially on the absurdity of accidental death. In Miss O'Connor's existential universe all events, including whatever acts of poetic justice the reader may happen to see, are essentially unpredictable, beyond human control, and, in a strict sense, accidental. It is only death, however, that speaks loudly enough to convince man of his foolish self-deceptions. "She was a talker, wasn't she?" says Bobby Lee, as The Misfit concludes his massacre of Bailey Boy's family by firing three slugs into its senior member. Underlining the major theme of the story, The Misfit rebukes his lieutenant: "Shut up, Bobby Lee. . . . It's no real pleasure in life."

Coming early in the story, the grandmother's anecdote of her dead beau Mr. Edgar Atkins Teagarden announces this theme of the vanity of human wishes and foreshadows the family's disastrous end:

> She said he was a very good-looking man and a gentleman and that he brought her a watermelon every Saturday afternoon with his initials cut in it, E. A. T. Well, one Saturday, she said, Mr. Teagarden brought the watermelon and there was nobody at home and he left it on the front porch and returned in his buggy to Jasper, but she never got the watermelon, she said, because a nigger boy ate it when he saw the initials, E. A. T.! This story tickled John Wesley's funny bone and he giggled and giggled but June Star didn't think it was any good. She said she wouldn't marry a man that just brought her a watermelon on Saturday. The grandmother said she would have done well to marry Mr. Teagarden because he was a gentleman and had bought Coca-Cola stock when it first came out and that he had died only a few years ago, a very wealthy man.

The watermelon, which neither Grandma nor Mr. Teagarden ever got to enjoy, and instead was inadvertently devoured by the Negro boy, symbolizes the sensual and specifically sexual gratifications allowed the Negro but denied the virtuous white man under the peculiar dispensations of the Protestant ethic. Her attitude of holding out for more than watermelon suggests June Star has been corrupted at an even earlier age than Pamela, while John Wesley's laughter punctuates Miss O'Connor's rather broad and heavy irony. Coca-Cola (as opposed to watermelon, an artificial gratification), which furnishes the basis of Mr. Teagarden's wealth, also provides a transition to the scene at Red Sammy's roadside barbecue-and-soft-drink tower that follows.

The irresistible hint that Red Sammy is the Devil or his agent gives the key both to his character and that of The Misfit, who to this point has remained only a sinister rumor. By pretending a flattering allegiance to the grandmother's radical and disastrous prejudice in favor of the past, Red Sammy is no mean contributor to the family's downfall. He is full of platitudes, lies, and diabolical half-truths. "These days you don't know who to trust," he says ironically, all the while calculating his take at the till. While a manifestly mercenary motive would explain this cajoling of his customers, hints of a darker purpose are plentiful. At its bottom reaches—and Red Sammy's is certainly that—both the physical exterior and psychological workings of capitalistic enterprise reveal its true ugliness and depravity. There is no need of a deeper hell or profounder hellishness. Sammy's wife says she wouldn't be surprised if The Misfit attacked their cash register. Taking up this suggestion of a harrowing of hell, the reader may prepare himself for the catastrophic and apocalyptic events that bring the story to its predicted conclusion.

The coming of The Misfit, which like the coming of Antichrist heralds the Last Day, is first rumored by the newspaper Grandma is reading as the narrative opens. Like Sammy's wife, the other characters pay religious lip service to the proximity of this terror partly to make topical conversation and partly to exorcise a real fear for their individual safety. They think of The Misfit as they think of death; and that indeed is one of the things he represents. Admirably designed as an agent of divine wrath, The Misfit is also, and less plausibly, presented as an existential Everyman. "I been most everything," he confides. "Been in the arm service, both land and sea, at home and abroad, been twict married, been an undertaker, been with the railroads, plowed Mother Earth, been in a tornado, seen a man burnt alive oncet. . . . but somewheres along the line I done something wrong and got sent to the penitentiary. I was buried alive" Playing shrewdly on the religious meanings of *penitentiary*, the story draws a Kafkaesque comparison between The Misfit's unremembered crime and original sin. When the grandmother placatingly suggests he might have been brought up on false charges, he declares:

"Nome . . . It wasn't no mistake. They had the papers on me." *Papers,* in this metaphorical instance, means Scriptural as well as legal proof. After scorning the old woman's further suggestion that his crime has been theft (the apple myth literally interpreted), he proceeds with his allegorical confessions: "It was a head-doctor at the penitentiary said what I had done was kill my daddy but I known that for a lie. My daddy died in nineteen ought nineteen of the epidemic flu and I never had a thing to do with it. He was buried in the Mount Hopewell Baptist churchyard and you can go there and see for yourself." No doubt a psychoanalyst, the head-doctor in question seems to have been imbued with Freud's theory that primitive man thought of original sin as parricide. While Freud announced this idea in "Totem and Taboo," its refinement in "Dostoevsky and Parricide" has greater relevance to the portrait of The Misfit, which is remarkably like Freud's subject in this latter essay.

According to Freud: "Dostoyevsky's condemnation as a political prisoner was unjust and he must have known it, but he accepted the undeserved punishment at the hands of the Little Father, the sin [a death wish] against his real father."[2] Like Dostoyevsky, who made "use of his sufferings as a claim to be playing a Christlike role," The Misfit also identifies himself with Jesus, claiming: "It was the same case with Him as with me except He hadn't committed any crime and they could prove I had committed one because they had the papers on me." Both the Freudian Dostoyevsky and The Misfit are depicted as sado-masochists, unable either to escape or wholly to accept their guilt; and both stoically refuse to allow science to explain it away. Attempting to cast further suspicion on the genuineness of Dostoyevsky's penitential experience in Siberia, Freud cites the novelist's sympathy with the criminality of his fictional characters, a feeling that "goes far beyond the pity which the unhappy wretch might claim, and reminds us of the 'holy awe' with which epileptics and lunatics were regarded in the past." For Dostoyevsky a criminal is "almost a Redeemer," Freud observes, "who has taken on himself the guilt which else must have been borne by others."[3] This last remark, which might apply to Stavrogin, Raskolnikov, or Dmitri Karamazov, serves equally well to describe Miss O'Connor's dramatic conception of The Misfit.

The intellectual quarrel between science and religion, allegorized in the anecdote of The Misfit's difference of opinion with the prison psychiatrist, can be resolved only by the individual's (prisoners's) flight from this world (the prison break) and his spiritual alienation. Isolated, even outlawed, he will either direct the violent longings of his soul inward (under conversion) or he will direct that violence, as The Misfit does, against others. The danger of secularism (the prison's psychiatrically oriented rehabilitation program) is that it attempts to rationalize man's inherent spiritual drives out of existence, rather than acknowledging and providing for them. Secularism makes war (the story contains several strategic reminders that World War II has not been long concluded) inevitable, for the psychology of nations or masses of people is identical with that of the individual in his search for spiritual—and sexual—release. As we have already seen from the example of Edgar Atkins Teagarden, capitalism sees to it that even man's baser needs (for watermelon) are not really satisfied. Psychoanalysis is thus on a par with Coca-Cola as an index of the ersatz character of modern civilization.

We now have to deal with Act Five, The Misfit's shooting of the grandmother, an incident that fits in with the desperate and perverse imitation of Christ we have noticed earlier. Having ordered the murder of Bailey Boy, whose unneeded shirt he now wears, The Misfit understandably reminds the dazed and fear-stricken old woman of her son: "Why you're one of my babies," she cries. As she reaches to touch him, The Misfit kills her. To his warped but alert intelligence, the grandmother's embrace represents an ancient threat to his identity. He is not Bailey Boy (the Old Adam), despite the fact that he is wearing Bailey's yellow shirt, decorated with blue parrots to indicate man's animal nature. Wearing the shirt means, emblematically, putting on the flesh, becoming incarnate. This final act of seemingly incomprehensible cruelty recalls Raskolnikov's nausea at his mother's physical approach as well as certain echoes from the Gospels.[4] By killing the old woman—again the reminder of *Crime and Punishment*—The Misfit asserts his spiritual independence from Dame Nature or Mother Earth. He is, emphatically, not one of her babies. Where the alternative to nonadjustment is Bailey Boy, one may agree that man does well to remain a "misfit."

Flannery O'Connor was, it is almost needless to say, an incorrigible allegorist, but one who was wise enough to see, as Hawthorne had, the necessity of rooting allegory in history. Her interpreter needs at the outset, therefore, a good firm grip on the obvious and literal significance of her plots before launching into an analysis of their symbolic aspects. The reader must equally go in fear of seeing too little as of finding too much in often very detailed physical descriptions of character. For example: Are the glasses The Misfit wears a "silent parable" that says in effect, We see through a glass darkly? Wherever such motifs recur through her work, as this one does, the initiate may exercise something like a confident judgment. Although doubtless familiar with the literary methods of Dante and of James Joyce, Miss O'Connor was very much her own writer. An insistence on paradigms, such as the four-fold manner of allegorical interpretation, as the key to her fiction will certainly lead to distortion rather than illumination. Any doctrinaire approach is likely, first of all, to neglect one of the major virtues of her style—the brutal satire one discovers so abundantly in "A Good Man Is Hard to Find." One safe rule of allegorical conduct is to remember that the true emblem participates in the reality its meaning temporarily transcends.

We see through a glass darkly only where there is real glass, and real darkness.

The blackness that Flannery O'Connor detected in the American soul, and that Hawthorne had found a century before, was in neither case mere literary invention. Despite her indebtedness to Hawthorne, as well as to Kafka and Joyce, she had, however, none of their moral uncertainty, and very little of the psychological insight that would induce such a skepticism. A graver deficiency or limitation of her work is that lifelessness of characterization that Hawthorne recognized as a frequent flaw in his own early productions. As Hawthorne further saw, it was only when the plight of his brainchildren touched their author's heart as well as his moral imagination that they took on the roundness and reality of the living flesh. It is not brilliance of invention one misses in "A Good Man Is Hard to Find," but something of real human dignity and "the mere sensuous sympathy of dust for dust."

Notes

1. *The Living Novel: A Symposium,* Granville Hicks, ed. (New York, 1957), 159.

2. Sigmund Freud, *Collected Papers* (London, 1953), 1, 233.

3. *Ibid.*, 237.

4. The Misfit reminds us too of Hamlet, whose extreme cruelty to Gertrude, while merely neurotic in the Freudian view, is also and primarily a defense of moral and spiritual values as against the claims of kinship and natural affection. Disagreeing with Freud, Rank and Jung revert to something like orthodoxy by insisting on Hamlet's reviling of his mother as part of a healthy and even heroic effort to establish his own identity; see Otto Rank, *The Myth of the Birth of the Hero and Other Writings* (New York, 1959), p. 302 and C. G. Jung, "The Battle for Deliverance from The Mother," in *Symbols of Transformation* (New York, 1956), II, 274–305.

WILLIAM S. DOXEY

A Dissenting Opinion of Flannery O'Connor's "A Good Man Is Hard to Find"

At the risk of having my garage burned (in lieu of a barn) by her faithful admirers, I am going to show why I am convinced that Flannery O'Connor's "A Good Man Is Hard to Find" is a flawed short story. This is not to say that the story is totally without merit. To the contrary, it has several redeeming features, one, from the teacher's standpoint, being the flaw itself. But just as one or two robins do not make a spring, so too an interesting character or fascinating event does not necessarily make a successful story. Before getting down to particulars, I must give my reasons for severely criticizing such a fine writer as the late Miss O'Connor. To be brief: "A Good Man Is Hard to Find" does not bear up under close analysis; *yet,* it has been praised in terms bordering upon adoration, and has been widely anthologized and purveyed to college students as a shining example of—well—symbolism—or something. The flaw in the story has led to many obtuse, confusing, and humorously contradictory judgments.

Now that my motivations are seen to be neither personal prejudice nor fanciful whim, I will get to the crux of the problem. "A Good Man Is Hard to Find" fails as a short story because of its structure. Specifically, the point-of-view shifts from the grandmother to The Misfit and the reader is suddenly

From *Studies in Short Fiction* 10 (1973): 199–204.

left holding the bag, as it were, or—to be more technical—without a focus of narration.

There are also other problems, but before looking at them I must anticipate certain objections. Yes, I fully understand that many reputable critics admire the structure of the story. For example, Miss Caroline Gordon "contemplated the structure" of the story "and found it written 'in the one way that is mathematically right—to borrow a phrase from James's notebooks."[1] Miss Gordon is also convinced that "A Good Man Is Hard to Find" has "perfection of phrasing."[2]

Well, maybe it does have "perfection of phrasing," whatever that is. But it does not have a consistent point of view. Who says it must? No one. In fact, even E. M. Forster, who is perhaps the wisest critic of the twentieth century, admits that a shifting viewpoint doesn't necessarily bother him, so long as it causes no confusion; but at the same time he cautions against a shift because too often it leads the writer into revealing too much interest in his method to the detriment of his story.[3]

But where does the alleged shift in viewpoint occur in "A Good Man Is Hard to Find," and what exactly are its consequences? The shift takes place soon after Bailey Boy loses control of the automobile and the family is plunged into the ditch. In the course of the preceding twelve pages (a total of twenty-one in the 1955 printing, or roughly fifty-seven percent), the reader is led through a series of misadventures that, taken altogether, characterize (one is tempted to use the prefix "over-") the family as being—well, what? Typical? Not exactly, yet—. One critic believes that "the whole story clearly illustrates the absence of love in the modern world, especially in family situations."[4]

Up to the moment at which the point-of-view changes, the family is, indeed, all we have to work with. They are driving to Florida for a vacation. Bailey Boy is behind the wheel, his wife and baby beside him on the front seat; the grandmother and the two children (and the grandmother's cat, which is hidden) are in the back seat. As the car rolls down the highway, we come to know these characters. Bailey Boy and his wife are rather dense, uncommunicative creatures; the two children are perfect brats (as they must be, for they are fated to be murdered and the reader's sympathy must not lie with them); the grandmother seems to have some refinement, but mainly she is concerned with having things her way. When the family stops for a bite at a roadside café, we meet Red Sammy Butts and his wife. It is Red Sammy who first observes that "a good man is hard to find." Some two and a half pages later the accident occurs, when the grandmother's cat leaps from concealment and distracts Bailey Boy.

Enter now from nowhere The Misfit, exit the point of view.

Of course, The Misfit does not come as a *complete* surprise. Early in the story he is mentioned as one reason for going to Tennessee rather than Florida by the grandmother, who has read in the paper of his escape from prison. And at Red Sammy's she speaks of him again. But all in all it seems a marvelous coincidence that he should suddenly appear in "a big black battered hearse-like automobile" on the very same deserted dirt road.

Whether the meeting be by coincidence, or by fate, or whatever one chooses to call it,[5] the rest of the story focuses on The Misfit; and, in the conclusion, we suddenly realize that we probably know (or think we know) more about him than the grandmother, whom initially we were led to accept as the main character. The Misfit shoots her, and the last word is his.

This, then, is the shift in point of view that I believe causes much confusion in understanding the story. But many critics see no difficulty and, consequently, feel that they understand the story perfectly. It is interesting to examine what they have to say, but first let us consider Miss O'Connor herself. If anyone should know what "A Good Man Is Hard to Find" is about, it logically seems she should. While discussing her work in 1963, she remarked that ". . . it is the free act, the acceptance of grace particularly, that I always have my eye on as the thing which will make the story work. In the story 'A Good Man Is Hard to Find,' it is the grandmother's recognition that The Misfit is one of her babies."[6] This idea of "grace" stems from her Catholic view, which also largely explains the grandmother's death (after receiving grace!), for Miss O'Connor states, "I'm a born Catholic [whatever that means] and death has always been brother to my imagination. I can't imagine a story that doesn't properly end in it or in its foreshadowing."[7] "A Good Man Is Hard to Find" ends rather emphatically in "it," for at the conclusion six corpses grace the Georgia landscape.

Returning now to the switch in viewpoint, we find that as a result The Misfit becomes the main interest. Coming as he does out of nowhere in the latter portion of the story, and strongly characterized as a grotesque figure, it is understandable that so many critics hold differing views of him. He is variously termed a Jesus figure, a murderer, an embodiment of evil, a good man, a Pascalian gambler, a lapsed idealist, a tragic figure, an agent of God, and a Hamlet *and* a Raskolnikov who becomes independent of nature.[8]

Well, can all of these sincere opinions be correct? Yes and no. Many are related in that they see The Misfit as a representative of "evil." Certainly, his murderous actions at the conclusion can hardly be taken as a manifestation of "good." Yet, one commentator feels that "the grandmother is engaged in a religious ordeal . . . the issue is not her mortal life, nor the lives of the invincibly ignorant members of her family, but her immortal soul," and finds that "despite all her ignoble efforts to save her own skin at all costs, despite her denying Him, He compassionately gives her a last chance."[9] With The Misfit? Some compassion! Possibly, this notion is what another critic is driving at when he says that the story ends "with some sense of elevation, something akin to the conclusion of the *Divine Comedy* in contrast to the nature of the preceding grim subject matter."[10] Perhaps, but it seems impossible to agree with another observer's contention that just before her death the grandmother "realizes that her superficial commitment to good has been meaningless because she lived without faith, that is to say without Christ."[11]

I wish I could also end as hopefully as Dante. But the story still sticks in my throat. In spite of all these critical observations presented in well-wrought prose and brilliant analogies, the point of view problem remains. To be honest, I once believed that the best explanation for this error was that Miss O'Connor either had two stories (one about the grandmother, the other about The Misfit) that she spliced together, or that she wrote the first part (up to the accident), put it aside, came back to it—perhaps by chance—several years later, and added The Misfit. These conjectures explained not only the point-of-view switch, but also the lack of proportion between The Misfit's large character and his slight foreshadowing.

That is what I used to believe. Now, however, I realize that there is another explanation for the great emphasis The Misfit receives; while it does not—*cannot*—fully justify the change in point of view, at least it gives a reason for Miss O'Connor's technical liberty. "Grace" is the key here, grace and the Catholic view of sin and good and evil. Ironically, "A Good Man Is Hard to Find" is a Catholic story by a "born Catholic" which imposes a Catholic view on decidedly non-Catholic characters. (I wonder, is it kosher to confront fundamentalist Protestant characters with Catholic theology?) In other words, "A Good Man Is Hard to Find" might best be considered an "inside" story understandable only to confirmed initiates. Miss O'Connor points to this idea when, after having mentioned the grandmother's "acceptance of grace" by recognizing that "The Misfit is one of her children," she discusses sin and freedom from the Catholic writer's standpoint: "The Catholic novelist believes that you destroy your freedom by sin; the modern reader believes, I think, that you gain it that way. There is not much possibility of understanding between the two."[12] And one paragraph later she makes this telling generalization: "In my stories a reader will find that the devil accomplishes a good deal of ground work that seems to be necessary before grace is effected."

Obviously, when a writer undertakes to deal with the devil her work is cut out for her. And when she chooses to dramatize the Catholic view of grace as well, she seems bound to confuse the uninformed. Explication then becomes exegesis and technical aspects are overlooked. But when one sees that the awareness of grace requires a face-to-face encounter with evil in all its malicious splendor, then he can understand the necessity for The Misfit (who represents this evil) to be strongly characterized. Once this point is established, one can comprehend—even though one may not condone—the consequent necessity for the author's taking liberties with technical aspects, such as, in the case of "A Good Man Is Hard to Find," point of view.

I must conclude, then, much in the same manner as a diplomat agreeing to a treaty which he knows is necessary, but which, for ingrained reasons, he cannot accept without admitting to himself that he is compromising his basic values. Regardless of what the reason, a shift in point of view in a short story *is* confusing, as I believe I have demonstrated. When one understands the reason for it, however, one might just be able to comprehend, at last, a story which till then has been, for some inexplicable reason, causing much confusion. Such, I am convinced, is the case with Miss O'Connor's "A Good Man Is Hard to Find."

Notes

1. Caroline Gordon, "An American Girl," in *The Added Dimension: The Art and Mind of Flannery O'Connor,* edited by Melvin J. Friedman and Lewis Lawson (New York: Fordham University Press, 1966), 127 [hereafter designated *The Added Dimension*]. Aside from causing me to wonder what mathematical system Henry James had in mind, this comment reveals that Miss Gordon knows James's notebooks and that's all. But she doesn't stop with that small praise of the structure of the story, for she pronounces that "A Good Man Is Hard to Find" is one of four of Miss O'Connor's stories that "nearly approach perfection," and that "when Miss O'Connor falls short of her best work, the flaw is always in the *execution* of the story, not in the *structure*" [*Ibid.,* 128, Miss Gordon's italics] James's "The Art of Fiction" looms large here; and while I would never deny the writer her *donnée,* I would suppose structure to be at least a part of execution, which is, of course, the aspect of the writing which, according to James, we may judge.

2. *Ibid.,* 135.

3. E. M. Forster, *Aspects of the Novel* (New York: Harcourt, Brace and World, 1954), 78–79.

4. Sister M. Bernetta Quinn, O. S. F., "Flannery O'Connor, A Realist of Distances," *The Added Dimension,* 174.

5. In her *Flannery O'Connor: Voice of the Peacock* (New Brunswick, New Jersey: Rutgers University Press, 1972), 72, Kathleen Feeley curiously explains The Misfit's strange entry: "So real are the events of the story that one can accept the metaphysical turn which the story takes when The Misfit enters."

6. Flannery O'Connor, "The Novelist and Free Will," *The Added Dimension,* 229.

7. C. Ross Mullins, "Flannery O'Connor: An Interview," *The Added Dimension,* 228.

8. Melvin J. Friedman, "Introduction," *The Added Dimension,* 18: The Misfit is "a murderer who likens himself to Jesus." Harold C. Gardner, S. J., "Flannery O'Connor's Clarity of Vision," *The Added Dimension,* 190: The Misfit is "the most obvious incarnation of evil" found in Miss O'Connor's work. Kathleen Feeley, *Flannery O'Connor: Voice of the Peacock,* 74: "Yet The Misfit is a 'good man' in many respects. The author draws him with compassion and puts him far ahead of Bailey and Red Sammy in gentleness and politeness." Irving Malin, "Flannery O'Connor and the Grotesque,"

The Added Dimension, 113; The Misfit "*will be the new Jesus of self-love*" [Malin's italics]. Frederick J. Hoffman, "The Search for Redemption," *The Added Dimension,* 41: The Misfit has a "distorted vision of the Pascalian wager." Sister M. Bernetta Quinn, O. S. F., "Flannery O'Connor, A Realist of Distances," *The Added Dimension,* 174: The Misfit is "like Chaucer's Pardoner . . . a fallen idealist." Carter W. Martin, *The True Country: Themes in the Fiction of Flannery O'Connor* (Nashville: Vanderbilt University Press, 1969), 230: The Misfit is "a tragic figure who struggles vainly against his own convictions." Brainard Cheney, "Miss O'Connor Creates Unusual Humor out of Ordinary Sin," *Sewanee Review* 71 (1963), 647: "God has made The Misfit of a secular world His agent. . . . Miss O'Connor has introduced God's charity nowhere more subtly, or more dramatically, than in . . . [this] disarming story." (But can the "subtle" be "dramatically" presented?) W. S. Marks, III, "Advertisements for Grace: Flannery O'Connor's 'A Good Man is Hard to Find," *Studies in Short Fiction* 4 (1966), 26: The Misfit "reminds us of Hamlet" as well as Raskolnikov; Marks goes on to say that when The Misfit kills the grandmother, he "assures his spiritual independence from Dame Nature or Mother Earth."

9. Cheney, 647–648.

10. Martin, 237.

11. Bob Dowell, "The Moment of Grace in the Fiction of Flannery O'Connor," *College English* 27 (1965), 236.

12. Flannery O'Connor, "The Novelist and Free Will," *The Added Dimension,* 229.

MICHAEL O. BELLAMY

Everything Off Balance: Protestant Election in Flannery O'Connor's "A Good Man Is Hard to Find"

Robert Milder's article, "The Protestantism of Flannery O'Connor," is based on two essential aspects of Protestantism he finds in O'Connor's so-called Catholic fiction: "The first is an insistence upon the absolute and irremediable corruption of the natural man, and consequently upon the necessity of divine grace for every good work; the second is an exaltation of private religious experience at the expense of the sacraments and the institutional Church." Late in his essay, Milder mentions that "A Good Man Is Hard to Find" is one of O'Connor's more Catholic stories.[1] I would like to take issue with Milder, not because of his association of O'Connor's writings with Protestantism, but rather because, at least in the case of "A Good Man," he does not go far enough. It is difficult to explain the crucial event in this story, the sudden and abrupt conversion of the grandmother, without reference to evangelical Protestantism. Moreover, The Misfit, the other major character in "A Good Man," is a visible manifestation of the theological contradictions which Milder describes in his discussion of O'Connor: much like his author, The Misfit is a Bible Belt

---

From *The Flannery O'Connor Bulletin* 8 (1979): 116–124.

Fundamentalist in spite of himself. Thus, we can learn something significant about this story in particular, as well as its author's more generally significant religious beliefs, by considering the extent to which "A Good Man" reveals the conflict between Flannery O'Connor's avowed Catholicism and her tendency to view religious experience in the context of Protestant Election.

On the most general level, the story has resonances of the typical spiritual allegory of the Protestant pilgrim. Once this overall similarity to the situation in, say, *Pilgrim's Progress,* is established, specific differences stand forth. The family in O'Connor's story is on a journey, but unlike the pilgrim in Bunyan's book, they are literally, and spiritually, on vacation; it is appropriate that they get lost, for, though they are headed for Florida in a sense, they are really going nowhere. O'Connor's story also differs from Bunyan's in that the entire family comes along; given the incessant bickering of the family in "A Good Man Is Hard to Find," it is obvious, in retrospect, why the pilgrim in *Pilgrim's Progress* who hopes to succeed must leave his family behind. The accident that ends with the automobile "in a gulch off the side of the road" is reminiscent of the "slough of despond" that temporarily interrupts the quest in *Pilgrim's Progress*. The crucial difference is that the family does not survive. Their executor, The Misfit, appears on the road above them in his "hearse-like" automobile, an Anti-Christ in his chariot, announcing the apocalypse. The Misfit's role as an Anti-Christ is subsequently maintained by other ironic inversions of divine characteristics. Unlike Christ, who suffered little children to come unto Him, the Misfit shuns John Wesley and June Star, for children make him "nervous." His reference to the fact that he "was a different breed of dog" from his brothers and sisters is similarly indicative of his satanic nature, for "dog" is, of course "God" spelled backwards, and demonology is based on inverting the sacred.

This set of inversions is consistent with The Misfit's entire personality, for he is a sort of Protestant exegetical scholar *manqué*. Temperamentally, he is suited for the kind of profound, sustained curiosity that motivates the biblical scholar. His father used to describe this trait in a down-to-earth way: "It's some that can live their whole life out without asking about it and it's others has to know why it is, and this boy is one of the latters. He's going to be into everything." The Misfit even looks like a scholar: "His hair was just beginning to gray and he wore silver-rimmed spectacles that gave him a scholarly look." Like many literal interpreters of the Bible, he has an inordinate respect for the written word. He does not, for example, question that he is guilty of the crime for which he was originally sent to prison, though he confesses he cannot recall exactly what he did. But never mind, he tells the grandmother: "It wasn't no mistake. They had the papers on me." For the original, but impossible, goal of tracking down his original sin, he has substituted the rectitude of keeping good records:

> He [Jesus] hadn't committed any crime and they could prove I had committed one because they had the papers on me. That's why I sign myself now. I said long ago, you can get a signature and sign everything you do and keep a copy of it. Then you'll know what you done and you can hold up the crime to the punishment and see do they match and in the end you'll have something to prove you ain't been treated right.

His interpretation of the prison psychiatrist's oedipal diagnosis is similarly indicative of exaggerated faith in the literal word. His literal understanding of Freud is but a secular correlative of a Fundamentalist reading of the Bible:

> It was a head-doctor at the penitentiary said what I had done was kill my daddy but I known that for a lie. My daddy died in nineteen ought nineteen of the epidemic

> flu and I never had a thing to do with it. He was burried in the Mount Hopewell Baptist churchyard and you can go there and see for yourself.

The Misfit is the man from Missouri who believes only in what he has seen; thus we learn immediately the difference between the grandmother's hypocrisy and his fidelity to his own experience when he corrects her version of the accident, stating that the car actually only turned over "oncet," for he had seen it happen. All he lacks is faith, for had be been there when Jesus "raised the dead," he would have immediately and radically changed his life:

> Jesus was the only One that ever raised the dead . . . and He shouldn't have done it. He thown everything off balance. If He did what He said, then it's nothing for you to do but thow away everything and follow Him, and if He didn't, then it's nothing for you to do but enjoy the few minutes you got left the best way you can—by killing somebody or burning down his house or doing some other meanness to him. No pleasure but meanness.

The central message of The Misfit's sermon, for a sermon is what his remarks amount to, is a familiar one in Flannery O'Connor's fiction; there is no middle ground between absolute belief in Christ's messianic function and a belief that life is nasty, brutish, and short. In fact, since The Misfit lacks faith in Christ's resurrection, he actually sees it as his duty to make life nastier, shorter, and more brutish. Implicit in the Manichean reduction of life to two antithetical alternatives is the Protestant insistence on man's total depravity without God's saving grace. The Misfit describes this belief as it applies to himself: "I found out the crime don't matter. You can do one thing or you can do another, kill a man or take a tire off his car, because sooner or later you're going to forget what it was you done and just be punished for it." The Misfit not only assumes that man in inherently guilty; he also assumes men are individually responsible for Original Sin. Given this congenital depravity, man is utterly incapable of doing anything to effect his own salvation. To do so would be roughly equivalent to pulling himself up by his own bootstraps. Here we have the surest sign of Protestantism: the absolute necessity of faith and, as a corollary, the belief that good works are at most merely a sign of God's favor.

The Misfit must be given credit for acting in conformity with his nature. We cannot say as much for the grandmother, for she is, until the moment of her death, a thorough hypocrite. It is of crucial importance that her election occurs at the very moment when she is at her most hypocritical. She has, in fact, just conceded—she will do anything to survive—that "maybe He [Christ] didn't raise the dead" after all. The moment of her election merits quoting at length:

> "Maybe He didn't raise the dead," the old lady mumbled, not knowing what she was saying and feeling so dizzy that she sank down in the ditch with her legs twisted under her.
>
> "I wasn't there so I can't say He didn't," The Misfit said. "I wisht I had of been there," he said, hitting the ground with his fist. "It ain't right I wasn't there because if I had of been there I would of known. Listen lady," he said in a high voice, "if I had of been there I would of known and I wouldn't be like I am now." His voice seemed about to crack and the grandmother's head cleared for an instant. She saw the man's face twisted close to her own as if he were going to cry and she murmured, "Why you're one of my babies. You're one of my own children!" She reached out and touched him on the shoulder. The Misfit sprang back as if a snake had bitten him and shot her three times through the chest. Then he put his gun down on the ground and took off his glasses and began to clean them.
>
> Hiram and Bobby Lee returned from the woods and

> stood over the ditch, looking down at the grandmother who half sat and half lay in a puddle of blood with her legs crossed under her like a child's and her face smiling up at the cloudless sky.

It is clear that the grandmother is a better woman at the moment of her death than she had been at any time heretofore; or, as The Misfit puts it, "She would of been a good woman if it had been somebody there to shoot her every minute of her life." The grandmother's salvation occurs when "her head cleared for an instant"; thus her legs, earlier described as "twisted" under her, are, subsequent to her salvation, "crossed under her like a child's." Similarly, for the first and only time, she imitates the rhetoric of the New Testament, not for her own selfish purposes, but because she actually feels a maternal concern for The Misfit as one of her own children.

The extraordinary thing about the grandmother's story is the radical discontinuity between her behavior and her redemption. In fact, this discontinuity is most apparent during the moments that immediately precede her conversion. How could the irrelevance of good works for salvation be more effectively demonstrated? How could there be any relationship between good works and election when it is the confrontation with death that brings about the moment of grace? Clearly, the grandmother will not be around for any good works, since her death is the occasion for her conversion.

There is another more explicit indication of the paradoxical relationship between merit and outcome in "A Good Man": The Misfit's very name is itself indicative of his inability to discover how his punishment fits his crime. This discontinuity is but the converse of the discrepancy between the grandmother's behavior and her extraordinary fate. If Christ has, in fact, "thown everything off balance" by overcoming death, His offer of salvation through grace has also disturbed the balance of the scales of justice. Again, broadly speaking, the imbalance implicit in the irrelevance of good works and the emphasis on the gift of faith is Protestant. The Misfit accepts this imbalance as the only conceivable interpretation of Christianity, even as he agonizes over the injustice of his own damnation. For without the gift of faith, The Misfit is inevitably unable to establish whether or not Christ actually rose from the dead: "It ain't right I wasn't there because if I had of been there I would of known. . . . Listen Lady, if I had of been there I would of known and I wouldn't be like I am now." Where, he asks, is the justice in a world in which grace is a gift, a gift he feels temperamentally incapable of receiving? Where is justice when the word "grace" actually means "favor"? For surely, by the very definition of the word, some people are "favored" or "gifted" and some are not.

This radical discontinuity between man's efforts and the divine gift of grace is the most obvious, and the most important, aspect of Flannery O'Connor's Protestantism. Again, the discontinuity is apparent in fates of both of the main characters in "A Good Man": The Misfit is genuinely concerned—in fact he is obsessed—with the ultimate issues of the human condition, while the grandmother, up to the very instant of her election, is a nauseating hypocrite. Thus, The Misfit's sincere efforts to investigate his place in the universe are to no avail, while the grandmother seems to stumble into salvation. Milder's comments on Protestantism are illuminating with respect to the fate of both characters. The attempt of The Misfit to understand his condition is bound to fail, for total depravity decrees "that man's reason has become so obscured since the Fall and his nature so debased that he is wholly incapable of virtue in his unregenerate state" (807). On the other hand, Milder's remarks on the grandmother are revealing to the extent that they tend to distort her experience. He sees "A Good Man" as one of O'Connor's more Catholic works in that the grandmother's election demonstrates "a free acceptance of grace," an aspect of the episode that Milder sees as "one of the few remaining doctrinal points which . . . [links Flannery O'Connor] to the Catholic tradition" (817). In the first place, it is obvious that "acceptance," free or otherwise, is not a very active word to describe the grandmother's role in the episode. Even at that, her will is barely apparent in what looks like a gratuitous gesture that is utterly antithetical to everything else in her life. In fact, her attempt to touch The Misfit is much like the existentialist's gratuitous act in its radical discontinuity from what went before. Given the doctrine of total depravity, election must be gratuitous, which is to say a gift given out of the context of the receiver's life. Thus, the grandmother is suddenly converted by an overwhelming infusion of grace, an experience much like St. Paul's abrupt enlightenment at the moment of his fall from his horse. What we have, in short, is Protestant election.

There are obvious aesthetic advantages to this kind of abrupt turn-about through a direct confrontation with God. The experience of election, as Milder perceptively points out, is far more likely to be dramatically moving than gradual spiritual improvement through the mediation of the sacraments or the practice of good works. But what is missing from the stunning conversion of the grandmother is the sense of balance, the sense of justice, so central to what Thomas Acquinas called the *via media*, or the middle way.[2] Acting in good faith is not, in this context, acting according to a specific body of doctrine, but rather the sort of endeavor The Misfit describes. He feels this kind of effort ought to be sufficient, but he does not believe it actually is. Conversely, the world in which the grandmother seems to be so arbitrarily saved, so far off the beaten track, or what we might call a middle way, does seem off-balance. The grotesque element that so many people have noted in O'Connor's fiction is in great part a result of this puzzling void between the few who seem to be somewhat arbitrarily saved, and just about everybody else, the depraved. This void is also a major feature of the surrealistic element in

O'Connor's fiction, that nightmarish quality that pervades the allegorical landscapes in which her grotesque figures engage in Manichean struggle. But if we step back from the works and view them in the context of their author's avowed beliefs, the most significant struggle is not this Manichean battle between good and evil, but rather the conflict between Flannery O'Connor's tendency to conceive of the human condition in terms of stark polarities, and the tendency, infrequently fulfilled but implicit in her Catholicism, to view mankind in the context of a middle way. It is because of this second attitude that the world of her fiction appears to The Misfit, to the Catholic humanist in Flannery O'Connor, and no doubt to many readers as well, as off-balance, almost at times in fact, as grotesque.

Notes

1. Robert Milder, "The Protestantism of Flannery O'Connor," *The Southern Review* 11 (1975), 802–819. The quote about Protestantism is on page 806; the reference to "A Good Man Is Hard to Find" is on page 817.

2. In fact, Milder also mentions this fundamental difference between Catholicism and Evangelical Protestantism (806–807).

WILLIAM J. SCHEICK

Flannery O'Connor's "A Good Man Is Hard to Find" and G. K. Chesterton's *Manalive*

In recent years critics have worked diligently to reveal the traditions informing Flannery O'Connor's writings. This undertaking has identified several influences on her fiction. Chief among these influences have been the Bible and various Christian thinkers ranging from Aquinas to Pierre Teilhard de Chardin and Jacques Maritain; and next in importance has been the heritage of Poe, Hawthorne, and James.[1] The heritage of the romance tradition, however, did not come to O'Connor simply from her American predecessors. The romance tradition flourished in England too, and among the writers in this tradition was Gilbert K. Chesterton, whose Christian perspective and fictional technique would have appealed to O'Connor. In fact, recently a critic cogently remarked the similarities between O'Connor's and Chesterton's views on romance and fantasy, although this critic only notes the similarities without suggesting Chesterton's possible influence and finally places O'Connor "among Hawthorne's following."[2]

As a major Catholic writer, Chesterton would have attracted O'Connor's attention, for in her letters and essays she frequently registered her interest in the subject of Catholic

From *Studies in American Fiction* 11 (1983): 241–245.

authors.[3] She apparently owned only one of Chesterton's books and she certainly did not refer to him often.[4] A notable instance of her interest in Chesterton, however, occurs in a letter (January 1, 1956), in which she indicates that she has not yet read Elizabeth Sewell's article on Chesterton printed in a current issue of *Thought*.[5] The scarcity of O'Connor's references to Chesterton has contributed to critical insensitivity to the possibility of his influence on her. Also contributing to this oversight is the general unfamiliarity with Chesterton's writings and the specific critical consignment of Chesterton's work to a small niche; both factors tend to obscure Chesterton's impact on such later significant authors as Jorge Luis Borges[6] and O'Connor, at least on O'Connor's "A Good Man Is Hard to Find."

The genesis of "A Good Man Is Hard to Find" has been traced to various news items in the *Atlanta Journal*.[7] The evidence for this origin is circumstantial, but enough particulars of congruence emerge to suggest that O'Connor might indeed have transformed in her story bits and pieces from various news accounts. Nevertheless, the most enigmatic moment in the story, The Misfit's conclusion that the grandmother "would have been a good woman . . . if it had been somebody there to shoot her every minute of her life," has no analog in the news accounts O'Connor read in the *Atlanta Journal*. Its origin appears to be Chesterton's *Manalive*.

Manalive recounts the strange adventures of Innocent Smith, "an allegorical practical joker,"[8] who

> seeks to remind himself, by every electric shock to the intellect, that he is still a man alive. . . . For this reason he fires bullets at his best friends; . . . he arranges ladders and collapsible chimneys to steal his own property; . . . he goes plodding round a whole planet to get back to his own home; . . . he has been in the habit of taking the woman whom he loved with a permanent loyalty, and leaving her about (so to speak) at

> schools, boarding-houses, and places of business, so that he might recover her again and again (368).

Often Smith's peculiar, "immature" behavior appears to be criminal, but in fact its "moral meaning . . . is concerned with an attempt to recover the lost sense of wonder and glamour of everyday life."[9]

The first of Smith's "crimes" or "jokes" most corresponds to The Misfit's behavior in "A Good Man Is Hard to Find." In this episode Emerson Eames, a student of Schopenhauer and a professor at the college Smith attends, concludes that life is not worth living: "A puppy with hydrophobia would probably struggle for life while we killed it; but if we were kind we should kill it. So an omniscient god would put us out of our pain" (211). Smith, with a characteristic lunacy which paradoxically makes rational sense, suddenly pulls a gun on Eames, who retreats toward a window. When he anxiously asks Smith, "Do you mean to kill me?", Smith replies, "It's not a thing I'd do for every one." As the only possible mode of escape from the maniac," Eames leaps out the window, clings precariously from a flying buttress, and cries for help:

> "The puppy struggles," said the undergraduate, with an eye of pity; "the poor little puppy struggles. How fortunate it is that I am wiser and kinder than he," and he sighted his weapon so as exactly to cover the upper part of Eames's bald head (215).

Smith fires two shots, but he deliberately misses Eames; for his purpose here, as it will be later when "he fires bullets at his best friends," is not to kill but "to bring him to life," to provide a "scare . . . so wholesome that the victim [will date] from it as from a new birth"; "All who had actually confronted the pistol confessed that they had profited by it" (226, 230).

Smith's effect on Eames corresponds to The Misfit's effect on the grandmother in O'Connor's story. An odd redeemer figure like Smith, The Misfit likewise expresses a paradoxically reasonable defense of his irrational behavior: "If [Jesus] did what He said, then it's nothing for you to do but thow away everything and follow Him, and if He didn't, then it's nothing for you to do but enjoy the few minutes you got left the best way you can—by killing somebody or burning down his house or doing some other meanness to him." Confronted by the reality of her imminent death, the grandmother at first despairs—"Maybe He didn't raise the dead"—and, passing through the dark night of the soul, comes to a sudden illumination about her kinship to The Misfit's manifestation of postlapsarian human nature—"You're one of my own children"—seconds before she is shot. As O'Connor has remarked about this scene: "The heroine of this story, the Grandmother, is in the most significant position life offers the Christian. She is facing death. And to all appearances she, like the rest of us, is not too well prepared for it," though finally "she makes the right gesture."[10] Death transforms the grandmother's postlapsarian childish selfishness into an image suggestive of a prelapsarian childlike innocence: "The grandmother . . . half sat and half lay in a puddle of blood with her legs crossed under her like a child's and her face smiling." The Misfit's remark, made while looking at the grandmother in this position, that she would have been a good woman if someone had shot her every minute of her life, recalls Innocent Smith's motivation for shooting at his friends: to make his life good for them every moment of their lives.

The similarities between Smith and The Misfit are striking. Equally noteworthy is Chesterton's and O'Connor's tendency to describe their characters in terms of animal imagery. This technique is ironic, finally, because both authors are emphatic in their respective works about the utter indifference of nature to all human plights. In Chesterton's novel, while Eames clings for his life on a flying buttress, "a bird alighting in his stone seat [takes] no more notice of him than of a comic statue" (219). In O'Connor's story, while the grandmother witnesses the murder of her family, "there [is] not a cloud in the sky nor any sun"; and after she is killed, "her face [smiles] up at the cloudless sky." Chesterton and O'Connor agree that nature offers humanity no answers to the riddle of life; only the end of life, each individual's experience of the apocalypse of death, can intimate life's meaning.

These similarities between Chesterton and O'Connor notwithstanding, their differences are equally striking. In fact the true merit of discovering Chesterton's influence on O'Connor's story lies in a recognition of how "A Good Man Is Hard to Find" apparently revises *Manalive*. O'Connor's short story does not merely derivatively reuse an episode in Chesterton's novel, but (as one would expect of a work by a major author like O'Connor) it thoroughly recasts this episode.

O'Connor's world is patently darker than Chesterton's. Innocent Smith shoots at but never wounds his friends; The Misfit kills his victims. Smith awakens others to the realization that life is worth living; The Misfit startles others into the realization that life is not worth living: "It's no real pleasure in life." Eames clings to life, while the grandmother eventually lets go of it. Moreover, Chesterton believes the threat of death can evoke an awareness tantamount to a new birth, whereas O'Connor remains ambiguous about the potentiality of death. The final image of the slain grandmother looking like a smiling child certainly recalls the scriptural passage about the necessity of becoming like a child before entering the kingdom of heaven, but it is only an image eliciting the reader's hope in the reality of Jesus' acts—the very crux of The Misfit's thoughts and actions. In O'Connor's story death is a release (the grandmother's smile) from the travail of life; whether it is just a release or whether it can signify a spiritual new birth remains a mystery, a matter of faith in each reader.

Innocent Smith (consciously) and The Misfit (unconsciously) evince the "new criminal incognito" of the "good man a little cracked." O'Connor apparently appreciated Chesterton's conception of Smith's use of violence in *Manalive;* however, she could not agree with the optimistic conclusions Chesterton derived from Smith's actions. In "A Good Man Is Hard to Find" she transformed the shooting episode in Chesterton's novel to reflect her darker sense of the nature of life. *Manalive* figured in the germinal stages of "A Good Man Is Hard to Find," which appears to be in part a deliberate revision of Chesterton's novel.

Notes

1. See, for example, Leon V. Driskell and Joan T. Brittain, *The Eternal Crossroads: The Art of Flannery O'Connor* (Lexington: University Press of Kentucky, 1971) and Sister Kathleen Feeley, *Flannery O'Connor: Voice of the Peacock* (New Brunswick: Rutgers University Press, 1972).

2. Marion Montgomery, "The Prophetic Poet and the Loss of Middle Earth," *Georgia Review* 33 (1979), 66–83.

3. See, for instance, Flannery O'Connor, *Mystery and Manners* (New York: Farrar, Straus, & Giroux, 1962).

4. Lorine M. Getz, *Flannery O'Connor: Her Life, Library and Book Reviews* (New York: Edwin Mellen Press, 1980), 90.

5. *The Habit of Being,* ed. Sally Fitzgerald (New York: Farrar, Straus, & Giroux, 1979), p. 126.

6. See Ronald J. Christ, *The Narrow Act: Borges' Art of Illusion* (New York: New York University Press, 1969), 113–130.

7. Victor Lasseter, "The Genesis of Flannery O'Connor's 'A Good Man Is Hard to Find,'" *Studies in American Fiction* 10 (1982), 227–232.

8. G. K. Chesterton, *Manalive* (London: Nelson, 1912), p. 166. Page references for subsequent quotations from this edition are identified parenthetically.

9. Ian Boyd, *The Novels of G. K. Chesterton: A Study in Art and Propaganda* (New York: Barnes and Noble, 1975), 55.

10. *Mystery and Manners,* 110, 112.

MADISON JONES

A Good Man's Predicament

Flannery O'Connor's "A Good Man Is Hard to Find" has been for the past decade or more a subject of virtually countless critical readings. Any brilliant work of fiction resists a single interpretation acceptable to everyone, but judging by the variousness and irreconcilability of so many readings of "A Good Man" one might conclude, as R. V. Cassill does, that like the work of Kafka the story "may not be susceptible to exhaustive rational analysis." The suggestion, I believe would be quite apt if applied to a good many O'Connor stories. Not this one, however. If there are in fact authorial lapses, moments when the reader's gaze is led a little awry, they are simply that, lapses, instances of O'Connor nodding.

Much has been made of O'Connor's use of the grotesque, and the vacationing family in "A Good Man" is a case in point. The family members are portrayed almost exclusively in terms of their vices, so much so, it would seem, as to put them at risk of losing entirely not only the reader's sympathy but even his recognition of them as representatively human—a result certain to drain the story of most of its meaning and power. Such is not the result, however. What otherwise must prompt severity in the reader's response is mitigated here by laughter, the transforming element through which human evil is seen in the more tolerable aspect of folly. The author laughs and so do we, and the moral grossness of the family becomes funny to us. This is what engages and sustains our interest in them and, through the effect of distance

From *The Southern Review* 20 (1984): 836–841.

that humor creates, makes possible our perception of their representative character.

What we see portrayed is increasingly recognizable. Here embodied in this family are standard evils of our culture. Indeed the term "family" it itself a misnomer, for there is no uniting bond. It is each for himself, without respect, without manners. The children, uncorrected, crudely insult their grandmother, and the grandmother for her own selfish ends uses the children against her surly son. The practice of deceit and the mouthing of pietisms are constants in her life, and her praise of the past when good men were easy to find degrades that past by the banality of her memories. Even such memories as she has are not to be depended on; in fact, it is one of her "mis-rememberings" that leads the family to disaster.

But this portrait of unrelieved vulgarity is extended, and by more than implication only, to suggest the world at large. This is the function of the interlude at Red Sammy's barbecue joint where the child June Star does her tap routine and Red Sammy bullies his wife and engages with the grandmother in self-congratulatory conversation about the awfulness of the times and how hard it is to find a "good" man these days. It is hard indeed. In a world unleavened by any presence of the spiritual—a world portrayed, incidentally, in scores of contemporary TV sit-coms—where is a good man to be found? Nowhere, is the answer, though in one way The Misfit himself comes closest to earning the description.

The Misfit is introduced at the very beginning of the story by the grandmother who is using the threat of him, an escaped convict and killer, as a means of getting her own way with her son Bailey. After this The Misfit waits unmentioned in the wings until the portrait of this representative family is complete. His physical entrance into the story, a hardly acceptable coincidence in terms of purely realistic fiction, is in O'Connor's spiritual economy—which determines her technique—like a step in a train of logic. Inert until now, he is nevertheless the conclusion always implicit in the life of the family. Now events produce him in all his terror.

The Misfit comes on the scene of the family's accident in a car that looks like a hearse. The description of his person, generally that of the sinister red-neck of folklore, focuses on a single feature: the silver-rimmed spectacles that give him a scholarly look. This is a clue and a rather pointed one. A scholar is someone who seeks to know the nature of reality and a scholar is what The Misfit was born to be. As The Misfit tells the grandmother:

> "My daddy said I was a different breed of dog from my brothers and sisters. 'You know,' Daddy said, 'it's some can live their whole life out without asking about it and it's others has to know why it is, and this boy is one of the latters. He's going to be into everything!'"

And in the course of his life he has been into everything:

> "I was a gospel singer for a while," The Misfit said. "I been most everything. Been in the arm service, both land and sea, at home and abroad, been twict married, been an undertaker, been with the railroads, plowed Mother Earth, been in a tornado, seen a man burnt alive oncet" . . . "I even seen a woman flogged," he said.

Life and death, land and sea, war and peace, he has seen it all. And his conclusion, based on his exhaustive experience of the world, is that we are indeed in the "terrible predicament" against which Bailey, who is about to be murdered for no cause, hysterically cries out. "Nobody realizes what this is," Bailey says, but he is wrong. The Misfit knows what it is: a universal condition of meaningless suffering, of punishment that has no intelligible relationship to wrongs done by the victim.

> "I call myself The Misfit," he said, "because I can't make what all I done wrong fit what all I gone through in punishment." . . . "Does it seem right to you, lady, that one is punished a heap and another ain't punished at all?" . . . "No lady." . . . "I found out the crime don't matter. You can do one thing or you can do another, kill a man or take a tire off his car, because sooner or later you're going to forget what it was you done and just be punished for it."

Now The Misfit signs everything and keeps a copy. That way:

> "You'll know what you done and you can hold up the crime to the punishment and see do they match and in the end you'll have something to prove you ain't been treated right."

The Misfit, of course, makes reference here to one significant experience not included in the catalogue previously quoted, but this experience was probably the crucial one. He was sent to the penitentiary for a crime—killing his father—of which he has no memory. In fact he is certain that he did not do it. But they had the papers on him. So, without any consciousness of the crime for which he was being punished, he was "buried alive," as he says. And his description of his confinement, with walls every way he turned, makes an effective image of The Misfit's vision of the world.

The penitentiary experience, however, has a further important thematic significance. It is the very figure of a cardinal doctrine of Christianity, that of Original Sin. Man, conscious or not of the reason, suffers the consequences of Adam's Fall. Guilt is inherited, implicit in a nature severed from God's sustaining grace and submitted to the rule of a Prince who is Darkness. Hence a world deprived of moral order, where irrational suffering prevails: the world that The Misfit so clearly sees with the help of his scholarly glasses.

Here, he believes, are the facts, the irremediable facts, of the human condition.

What The Misfit cannot see, or cannot believe in, is any hope of redress for the human condition. He may be haunted, at times tormented, by a vision of Christ raising the dead, but he cannot believe it: he was not there. All that he can believe, really believe, is what his eyes show him: this world without meaning or justice, this prison house where we are confined. Seeing this, what response is fitting? Says The Misfit:

> "Then it's nothing for you to do but enjoy the few minutes you got left the best way you can—by killing somebody or burning down his house or doing some other meanness to him. No pleasure but meanness," he said and his voice had become almost a snarl.

It is like the response of Satan himself, as Milton envisions it:

> Save what is in destroying; other joy
> To me is lost.

But release for hate of an unjust creation is at best an illusory pleasure. "It's no real pleasure in life," The Misfit says, after the carnage is complete.

What has driven The Misfit to his homicidal condition is his powerful but frustrated instinct for meaning and justice. It may be inferred that this same instinct is what has produced his tormenting thoughts about Christ raising the dead, making justice where there is none. If only he could have been there when it happened, then he could have believed.

> "I wish I had of been there," he said, hitting the ground with his fist. "It ain't right I wasn't there because if I had of been there I would of known. Listen lady," he said in a high voice, "if I had of been there I would have known and I wouldn't be like I am now."

It is torment to think of what might have been, that under other circumstances he would have been able to believe and so escape from the self he has become. In light of this it is possible to read The Misfit's obscure statement that Jesus "thown everything off balance," as meaning this: that it would have been better, for the world's peace and his own, if no haunting doubt about the awful inevitability of man's condition ever had been introduced. In any case it could only be that doubt has made its contribution to the blighting of The Misfit's soul.

But doubts like this are not enough to alter The Misfit's vision. In the modern manner he believes what he can see with his eyes only, and his eyes have a terrible rigor. It is this rigor that puts him at such a distance from the grandmother who is one of the multitude "that can live their whole life without asking about it," that spend their lives immersed in a world of platitudes which they have never once stopped to scrutinize. This, his distinction from the vulgarians whom the grandmother represents, his honesty, is the source of The Misfit's pride. It is why, when the grandmother calls him a "good" man, he answers: "Nome, I ain't a good man," . . . "but I ain't the worst in the world neither." And it is sufficient reason for the violent response that causes him so suddenly and unexpectedly to shoot the grandmother. Here is what happens, beginning with the grandmother's murmured words to The Misfit:

> "Why, you're one of my babies. You're one of my own children!" She reached out and touched him on the shoulder. The Misfit sprang back as if a snake had bitten him and shot her three times through the chest.

Given The Misfit's image of himself, her words and her touching, blessing him, amount to intolerable insult, for hereby she includes him among the world's family of vulgarians. One of her children, her kind, indeed!

This reason for The Misfit's action is, I believe, quite sufficient to explain it, even though Flannery O'Connor, discussing the story in *Mystery and Manners*, implies a different explanation. The grandmother's words to The Misfit and her touching him, O'Connor says, are a gesture representing the intrusion of a moment of grace. So moved, the grandmother recognizes her responsibility for this man and the deep kinship between them. O'Connor goes on to say that perhaps in time to come The Misfit's memory of the grandmother's gesture will become painful enough to turn him into the prophet he was meant to be. Seen this way, through the author's eyes, we must infer an explanation other than my own for The Misfit's action. This explanation would envision The Misfit's sudden violence as caused by his dismayed recognition of the presence in the grandmother of a phenomenon impossible to reconcile with his own view of what is real. Thus The Misfit's act can be seen as a striking out in defense of a version of reality to whose logic he has so appallingly committed himself.

Faced with mutually exclusive interpretations of a fictional event, a reader must accept the evidence of the text in preference to the testimonial of the author. And where the text offers a realistic explanation as opposed to one based on the supernatural, a reader must find the former the more persuasive. *If* the two are in fact mutually exclusive. And *if*, of course, it is true that the acceptability of the author's explanation does in fact depend upon the reader's belief in the supernatural. As to this second condition, it is a measure of O'Connor's great gift that the story offers a collateral basis for understanding grace that is naturalistic in character. This grace may be spelled in lower case letters but the fictional consequence is the same. For sudden insight is quite within the purview of rationalistic psychology, provided only that there are intelligible grounds for it. And such grounds are present in the story. They are implicit in the logic that connects the grandmother and The Misfit, that makes of The Misfit "one of my own children." In the hysteria caused by the imminence of her death, which strips her of those banalities by which she has lived, the grandmother quite believably discovers this connection. And so with the terms of The Misfit's sudden violence. His own tormenting doubt, figured in those preceding moments when he cries out and hits the ground, has prepared him. Supernatural grace or not, The Misfit in this moment sees it as such, and strikes.

These two, the author's and my own, are quite different explanations of The Misfit's sudden violence. Either, I believe, is reasonable, though surely the nod should go to the one that more enriches the story's theme. *If* the two are mutually exclusive. I believe, however, that they are not. Such a mixture of motives, in which self-doubt and offended pride both participate, should put no strain on the reader's imagination. And seen together each one may give additional dimension to the story.

"A Good Man Is Hard to Find" is perhaps Flannery O'Connor's finest story—coherent, powerfully dramatic, relentless, and unique. In essence it is a devastating sermon against the faithlessness of modern generations, man bereft of the spirit. This condition, portrayed in the grossness of the vacationing family, barely relieved by the pious and sentimental prattle of the grandmother, produces its own terror. The Misfit enters, not by coincidence but by the logic implicit in lives made grotesque when vision has departed. He, O'Connor tells us, is the fierce avenger our souls beget upon our innocent nihilism.

CARTER MARTIN

"The Meanest of Them Sparkled": Beauty and Landscape in Flannery O'Connor's Fiction

"'We've had an ACCIDENT,'" the children cry gleefully. "'But nobody's killed,' June Star said with disappointment." Within a few minutes, June Star is dead, and so is the rest of her family. The extraordinary irony informs the story in several ways. Like Eliot being surprised that so many have crossed the bridge or Ransom's characters being astonished at a child's death, we as readers of "A Good Man Is Hard to Find" are awed by the swiftness and finality of the six deaths effected by The Misfit. I think we come back to the story time and again to experience this awe and to inquire into it. We are, in this, somewhat like Mrs. Greenleaf [in O'Connor's story "Greenleaf"], who clips stories of grotesque deaths and bizarre suffering so that she can wallow in the dirt and pray over them. There is a medieval quality about the centrality of death in O'Connor's fiction.

There are, however, other dimensions to the irony of "A Good Man Is Hard to Find," specifically, that the automobile accident and the swift deaths following it constitute an opening up, a movement of this fiction to a moment when Flannery

---

From *Realist of Distances: Flannery O'Connor Revisited*, ed. Karl-Heinz Westarp and Jan Nordby Gretlund (Aarhus, Denmark: Aarhus University Press, 1987), 147–159.

O'Connor shows us, as she so often does, the landscape of eternity. Rather than showing us, as Eliot does, "Fear in a handful of dust," she shows us *beauty* in the most horrible of human experiences. This journey of the imagination from the horrible to the truth of God's grace has been an important response often noted by O'Connor's readers. Nevertheless, there is a wallowing in the dirt about it all, for we too often assume that it is only through the ugly and the grotesque, through suffering and pain, through loss and death that the grand truths of the universe emerge from *Wise Blood, A Good Man Is Hard to Find, The Violent Bear It Away,* and *Everything That Rises Must Converge*. However, O'Connor presented the beauty of this world as vividly as sunlight through the stained-glass window of a Gothic cathedral or the brilliant icons of the churches of Byzantium. It is this beauty I want to show in its importance in the total perception of O'Connor's fiction. It is one reason for her popularity—not just among academics but among readers everywhere of every persuasion and personal circumstance.

In his introduction to *Everything That Rises Must Converge,* Robert Fitzgerald took issue with those who complained that O'Connor's fiction "lacked a sense of natural beauty and human beauty." In refutation, Fitzgerald cites a line from a beautiful story, which is actually also O'Connor's most notoriously violent story, "A Good Man Is Hard to Find." The line reads: "The trees were full of silver-white sunlight and the meanest of them sparkled." More generally but relevant to this passage, Fitzgerald says: "Beyond incidental phrasing and images, beauty lies in the strong invention and execution of the things, as in objects expertly forged or cast or stamped, with edges, not waxen and worn or softly moulded." For this quality he uses the term *ascesis* because of its economy, its spareness and brevity. Further, he contends that the wife in "A Good Man Is Hard to Find" carries out a beautiful action when she politely says "Yes, thank you" to her murderer, as he leads her way into the woods. Such actions, he contends, are beautiful, "though as brief as beautiful actions usually are."

In spite of Fitzgerald's pointing the way, too little has been written about the very real beauty to be found in O'Connor's fiction. She herself does not use the word often, but in her nonfiction she makes it clear that beauty is very important to her view of the world. In a letter to "A" she states: "I am one, of course, who believes that man is created in the image and likeness of God. I believe that all creation is good" (p. 104). And when reviewers failed to see that there was (according to her) no bitterness in her stories but a cherishing of the world, she took their failure to be a moral one and tantamount to "what Nietzsche meant when he said God was dead" (p. 90). She admits that her stories in *A Good Man Is Hard to Find* contain "many rough beasts now slouching toward Bethlehem to be born," but contends that reviewers have "hold of the wrong horror." She insists that "you have to cherish the world at the same time that you struggle to endure it" (p. 90).

I want to demonstrate in several of O'Connor's works a pattern of beauty which I take to be an important part of the rhetorical structure of her fiction. These patterns happen to be at one with the narrative structure, and they are at one with her own statements in regard to what the works are "about." She once complained in a letter to Sister Mariella Gable that critics too often do not see what is really there, and she invoked Gerard Manley Hopkins's notion of "inscape" to explain what she meant (p. 517). Her method is at one with so many other writers who have, like Hopkins, written in 'Pied Beauty' about:

> All things counter, original, spare, strange;
> Whatever is fickle, freckled (who knows how?)
> With swift, slow; sweet, sour; adazzle, dim.

It is a method of indirection that nevertheless is especially about the beautiful. One thinks of Emily Dickinson, who spoke of this matter in one of her poems:

> Tell all the truth but tell it slant—
> . . . The truth must dazzle gradually,
> or every man be blind—

She carries out what Robert Browning's painter "Fra Lippo Lippi" claimed was one of the artist's functions:

> . . . We're made so that we love
> First when we see them painted, things we have passed
> Perhaps a hundred times nor cared to see. . . .
> Art was given for that . . .

O'Connor was herself a visual artist as well as a literary one. Robert Fitzgerald describes some of this graphic art: "They are simple but beautiful paintings of flowers in bowls, of cows under trees, of the Negro house under the bare trees of winter." Her literary work is also highly visual, and when this visualization is specifically beautiful it often constitutes a special form of punctuation that gives rhythm and shape to the structure of her narrative. One must look carefully to appreciate this aesthetic, for it is similar to what Auden perceives about Breughel and the old masters in his poem "Musée des Beaux Arts": Those painters understood, he says, the human position of suffering.

> How it takes place
> While someone else is eating or opening a window or
> just walking dully along. . . .
> That even the dreadful martyrdom must run its course
> Anyhow in a corner, some untidy spot
> Where the dogs go on with their doggy life and the torturer's horse
> Scratches its innocent behind on a tree.

The beauty in O'Connor's stories is that way: it occurs casually, is understated, characterized by the spareness of *ascesis,* and is usually surrounded by ugliness, banality, or violence. The result, however, is not necessarily an impression that beauty is chimerical or accidental but instead that it is the reality that informs the entire structure of the effective world she portrays. "For the almost blind," she wrote, "you draw large and startling figures." (*Mystery and Manners,* p. 34). Which is to say that she, like Dickinson, doubted the capacity of her audience to look directly and consistently upon the beauty that she herself perceived in the universe. Breughel's "The Blind People" portrays in the foreground a single file of stumbling, wildly disoriented blind men; but in the background landscape is the church. The rhetoric could not be simpler or clearer. In his "The Fall of Icarus" the rhetoric is similar; the great tragic drowning is proportionately minuscule in comparison to the coarse farmer, his ox and plow cutting fresh furrows in the foreground. In "The Hunters in the Snow" Breughel creates unusual beauty from a severe, colorless and cold landscape by investing it with meaning that comes from the shape of life and activity and the sense of returning home or coming into the open. The village and the frozen lake lie below the men and their slender dogs. . . .

When a reader enters an O'Connor story by looking through such windows that open onto beauty—particularly when he feels that the narrative house from which he looks is filled with darkness and terror and malignity—he is experiencing what Martin Heidegger refers to as "coming into the open." Heidegger asserts that "Meaning is . . . not a property attaching to entities, lying 'behind' them, or floating somewhere as an 'intermediate domain.'" It is the field upon which "something becomes intelligible as something."[1] Heidegger contends that the poet experiences the abyss (the "default of God," he calls it) and causes readers to reach into the abyss to discover divine radiance shining "in everything that is" and also to realize that absence is presence, "the ancient name of Being." In "What are Poets For?" Heidegger says that they "sense the trace of fugitive gods" and trace for others the way toward the turning. In the midst of the unholy, he claims, the songs of the venturesome poets (those who take dangerous risks) turn "our unprotected being into the Open."[2]

A reader's experience of coming into the open by way of O'Connor's punctuation of beauty is more elaborately realized in one of her most violent and disturbing stories, "A Good Man Is Hard to Find." The pattern of this story is a series of scenes in confined space which are seen in the context of unbounded space—light, sky, clouds, and woods seen from above so that they stretch out as the blue tops of trees. The story moves from the unpleasant circumstances of three-generational family life to the awesome absence of the lives so recently present. Yet this movement is one that leads us from the beauty of the world to the beauty of death or perhaps to the beauty of grace attendant upon death. The key lines form an image cluster that controls this meaning. Significantly, the perception originates with the grandmother, just as the presence of grace is understood only with reference to her at the time of the mass murder. When the family is setting out on their Florida trip, the grandmother tries to share the beauty she sees with the ill-tempered children, John Wesley and June Star:

> She pointed out interesting details of the scenery: Stone Mountain; the blue granite that in some places came up to both sides of the highway; the brilliant red clay banks slightly streaked with purple; and the various crops that made rows of green lace-work on the ground. The trees were full of silver-white sunlight and the meanest of them sparkled.

All of these images are patently beautiful: the mountain, the granite, the red clay, the crops, the trees, the sunlight, and in the combination that O'Connor places them, they are poetic and constitute a potential vortex, a radiant node or cluster into which the meaning of the story eventually enters. Only five of the twenty-one pages of the story do not contain cognate imagery. Even though we do not perceive it as beauty as it casually occurs, this imagery represents the macrocosm of the story and permits the reader to come into the open thematically on what O'Connor calls elsewhere "the true country." The fleeting signs of the reality of that country are in this story the woods filled with light, beginning with the grandmother's paean and moving through the chinaberry tree at Red Sammy Butts's, the "blue tops of trees for miles around," trees that look down on the family car, "woods, tall and dark and deep," "woods [that] gaped like a dark open mouth," and the woods that relentlessly devour the family before the awestruck grandmother: "Alone with The Misfit, the grandmother found that she had lost her voice. There was not a cloud in the sky nor any sun. There was nothing around her but woods." At this point the story has moved from the circumstantial beauty of the affective world to the ideal and permanent beauty of the action of grace that paradoxically informs the irrational gesture in which the grandmother reaches out to touch The Misfit, anagogically accepting him as her own, as Christ accepted sinners.

This remarkable conclusion to the story has been explained by O'Connor herself in terms of grace and its focus on the grandmother, but her explanation is not easy for many readers who see in the foreground a homicidal maniac carrying out a mass murder. However, if the reader examines the structure of the story, the affirmation of this reading is more available, even to the reader who may be unfamiliar with O'Connor's explanation. The pattern already described is enhanced by its contrapuntal movement with reference to the imagery of enclosure. The grim, threatening quality of the story begins before the appearance of The Misfit and is associated with the microcosm of the family, specifically as they are presented enclosed and entrapped, so confined and relentlessly bound to each other's presence that, except for the grandmother, they are unable to look out to the larger world or to conceive of the possibility that they may come into the open, enter a larger, freer, more beautiful world.

The first of these enclosures is the home itself. Only one and one-half pages long, it is a tightly blocked stage setting which conveys the maddening intimacy of family life. Bailey, the father, is unsuccessfully trying to escape by immersing himself in the sports section of the *Journal*. The garrulous grandmother is invading everyone's space by fatuously claiming a role as wise elder, warning the family of The Misfit and trying to change the plans for the trip to Florida; that she is expressing her desperate lack of belonging, of being an unwanted outsider is borne out by the cruel remarks of the children, who are lying on the floor reading the funny papers: "Why dontcha stay at home?" one of them asks. The mother, "whose face was as broad and innocent as a cabbage," sits on the sofa in quiet desperation, feeding apricots to the baby. The terrible proximity of them all creates an atmosphere of hysteria, and the reader's inclination is to scream and flee. This first instance of enclosure is brief and quite intense.

The enclosure in the automobile is similarly cloying because of the quite raw conflicts between the generations: a lonely and silly old woman trying to be cheerful and agreeable, children who are by turns ill-mannered or sullenly oblivious, and parents who are almost stupefied and overtaxed by their role as the responsible adults. They are caged and baffled in a rolling domestic zoo, objectified with satire and irony by the grandmother's stories, the children's cloud game, the baby being passed to the back seat, and occasional glimpses of the quickly passing stable world outside the car, one of which, the

Negro child, the grandmother would like to bring into stasis: "If I could paint, I'd paint that picture," she says. The overwhelming irony of the boredom and tension is that the end of it in the affective world is not reconciliation or a coming into love and harmony but sudden death.

The same ironic pathos informs the details of the third objectification of the existential enclosure of life in the countryside or the fallen world. Red Sammy Butts's restaurant, "The Tower was a long dark room with a counter at one end and tables at the other and dancing space in the middle." The discontent and hostility continue: Bailey glares at his mother when she asks him to dance, June Star insults Red Sammy's wife, he tells his wife "to quit lounging on the counter and hurry up with these people's order." The conversation is premonitory and pessimistic in its concern with The Misfit and the degeneration of mankind in general. It is a relief when "the children ran outside into the white sunlight and looked at the monkey in the lacy chinaberry tree."

The next narrative block returns to the enclosure of the automobile. It is at this time that the grandmother awakens "outside of Toombsboro" (note the extension of the irony and the imagery) with her plan to visit an old plantation, the venture that leads them to their encounter with The Misfit. The children are eager to get out of the car. The imagery of the secret panel and hidden silver and the sudden emergence of the cat from its basket foreshadow the sudden and catastrophic opening up of the narrative and of the six lives.

With the grandmother, the reader is awed by the ten-page conclusion to the story, more than one-third of its length. O'Connor protracts this event. She has prepared us for it carefully, so that when we see the hearselike car on the hill and look down upon the family spilled out from their banal entrapment into the big world, we know the terrible outcome at once. Thus we must participate in the moment of dying, with horror, outrage, and finally with wonder. This narration is somewhat like the medieval drama *Everyman* in which the protagonist's moment of death is expanded artistically and dramatically to include his realization, his pleading, his acceptance, and his receiving the sacraments and God's grace. A similar effect is achieved by Tolstoy in "The Death of Ivan Ilyich" and by William Faulkner in his treatment of the death of Joe Christmas in *Light in August*. To stand for so long before the mystery of death enables the reader to realize the irrelevance of the banality, the tension, the petty egotism and pride which constitute the ordinary life in physical and metaphysical confinement. This we are made aware of by the events at large and by passages of humbly apocalyptic beauty: "There was a pistol shot from the woods, followed closely by another. Then silence. The old lady's head jerked around. She could hear the wind move through the tree tops like a long satisfied insuck of breath. 'Bailey Boy!' she called." That the grandmother's action of reaching out to The Misfit signifies the moment when grace is manifest is a received truth about the story. It is not, however, a surprise ending. Her identity with grace occurs early and at several points before this conclusion. Coming into the open is clearly part of the story's structure and imagery, and part of the grandmother's character. We see this, for example, after the others have been taken away; she is alone with The Misfit and O'Connor confirms in this penultimate moment her having come into the open: "There was not a cloud in the sky nor any sun. There was nothing around her but woods. She wanted to tell him that he must pray. She opened and closed her mouth several times before anything came out. Finally she found herself saying, 'Jesus. Jesus,' meaning, Jesus will help you. . . ." Again the imagery of clouds, sky, sun, and trees objectifies beauty, spare and stark though it be; the end thus returns to the beginning image of the meanest trees filled with light. . . .

Notes

1. Martin Heidegger, *Being and Time*, trans. John Macquarrie and Edward Robinson (New York, 1962), 193.

2. Martin Heidegger, *Poetry, Language, Thought*, trans. and with Introduction by Albert Hofstaadter (New York, 1971), 174, 93, 94, 140.

J. PETER DYSON

Cats, Crime, and Punishment: *The Mikado's* Pitti-Sing in "A Good Man Is Hard to Find"

If the grandmother is, as she appears to be, the "good man" who is so hard to find in Flannery O'Connor's story, "A Good Man Is Hard to Find," then who or what, one wonders, is Pitty Sing, the grandmother's cat? Her namesake is of course one of the "Three Little Maids from School" who come tripping on-stage early in Act I of Gilbert and Sullivan's operetta *The Mikado*.[1] The connection between Pitti-Sing and Pitty Sing might not appear to be worth following up but for two reasons: the first is the nature of the fiction O'Connor was writing at this stage of her career; the second, growing out of the first, is that O'Connor herself seems clearly to reinforce the connection of the names by making one of the key utterances in her tale a clear echo of the best-known sentence from W. S. Gilbert's sardonic libretto. The Mikado explains himself and his conception of justice to his subjects by announcing, "My object all sublime / I shall achieve in time— / To let the punishment fit the crime— / The punishment fit the crime" (382). The Misfit attempts to explain *himself* and the way, in his view, justice functions, to the bewildered grandmother by saying: "I call myself The Misfit because I can't make what all I done wrong fit what all I gone through in punishment."

Few commentators on the story have had anything to

From *English Studies in Canada* 14 (1988): 436–452.

say about Pitty Sing, and those that have have been less than helpful. Puzzlement is the usual response; ignorance of, or generalized comment on, the connection with *The Mikado* character the norm.[2] Josephine Hendin, the major commentator to date on Pitty Sing, may be taken as representative of how far interpretation of the cat's function in the tale has gone. "The meaning of the cat," she writes, "seems to derive precisely from its symbolic thinness. That a pet, a cat, leaping at random for no great reason, should cause the destruction of an entire family expresses the randomness, the pointlessness of the murders."[3] Life, and indeed cats, may be random, but O'Connor as a writer, especially at this stage of her career, was emphatically not. Reading *Wise Blood,* written about the same time though published a year earlier, one feels that if it has a fault as a novel it is the almost excessively logical density of its symbolic texture. Only an insensitive reader could miss the precisely crafted significance of individual props (for example, Haze's Jesus-seeing hat, the potato-peeling machine, or, indeed, the mummy, revealed in the fullness of time and plot as the new Jesus of the Church of Christ without Christ) and the ingenious intricacy of the roles these props are called on to play or the interlocking system of character-doubling which underpins, with almost too cerebral a clarity, the fictional structure. "Symbolic thinness," "random," and "pointless" are inappropriate terms to apply to O'Connor's fictional technique in this tale which shares many of *Wise Blood's* characteristics.

I am less interested in "proving" sources than in following up some of the numerous and complex *Mikado* echoes in "A Good Man Is Hard to Find," letting them throw what light they can; the fact that the light is considerable is less surprising than one might suppose. The priorities of this paper preclude an extended discussion of Gilbert's libretto, the best-known of course among many, but, to a reader familiar with both, it is obvious that important aspects of its technique—the hardness of its intellectual structure and its witty brilliance—

are manifest in O'Connor's early fiction. Utilizing the major elements of wit—paradox, reversals of language and action—both works explore thematically the significance of the mysteriously arbitrary design by which characters and situations are moved despite themselves. But while Gilbert's all-powerful Mikado figure is deployed along his happily despotic way for purposes of social satire, the vagaries of human pretension are exploited by O'Connor as the material for a blackly comic exploration of the terrifying nature of Providence.[4] A clue to that nature is provided by the epigraph to the volume *A Good Man Is Hard to Find,* a feature of the story to which I shall return.

The primary usefulness of Pitty Sing, the connector between the two works, is to illuminate the roles of The Misfit and the grandmother in the O'Connor story; nevertheless, it is more useful to begin with a broader perspective. The best starting-point for seeing how the road coming out of the town square of Titipu leads structurally to the back roads of Georgia is the Mikado himself. Five minutes into the first act we learn that this supreme, arbitrary law-giver had paradoxically begun his reign by introducing a law with a purportedly educative purpose. Intended as "A plan whereby / Young men might best be steadied," it has succeeded in nothing but handing the kingdom over to absurdity and reducing the idea of law to a mockery. The "crime" is flirting, the punishment, beheading: "Our great Mikado, a virtuous man, / When he to rule our land began, / Resolved to try / A plan whereby / Young men might best be steadied. / So he decreed in words succinct, / That all who flirted, leered or winked / (Unless connubially linked), / Should forthwith be beheaded" (347–348).

The absurd law begets a correlative absurd response, reductive in nature, from the affected townspeople: "And I expect you'll all agree / That he was right to so decree. / And I am right, / And all is right as right can be!" (348). The law is a great leveller since everyone in Titipu is equally affected, but it is the young who suffer most: " The youth who winked a roving eye, / Or breathed a non-connubial sigh, / Was thereupon condemned to die— / He usually objected" (348).

Well might the youth of Titipu cry out with the voice of The Misfit, "I call myself The Misfit because I can't make what all I done wrong fit what all I gone through in punishment." However, The Misfit's perception of the irrationality of punishment is more thoroughgoing since it draws out the Mikado's logic one step further: If the severity of punishment is pushed beyond all logical correlation, then all crimes take on the same moral weight. His reply to the grandmother's question about what he did to get sent to the penitentiary the first time makes the point unmistakably: "I forget what I done, lady. . . . I found out the crime don't matter. You can do one thing or you can do another, kill a man or take a tire off his car, because sooner or later you're going to forget what it was you done and just be punished for it."

The final stanza of the song about the Mikado's law introduces a new character, Ko-Ko, whose career finds an astonishing echo in that of The Misfit. The townspeople of Titipu had taken counter-action against the threat of near-universal decapitation: "And so we straight let out on bail, / A convict from the county jail, / Whose head was next / On some pretext / Condemned to be mown off, / And made *him* Headsman, for we said, / 'Who's next to be decapitated / Cannot cut off another's head / Until he's cut his own off" (348). Ko-Ko, the "cheap tailor" (349), released in order to be appointed headsman, becomes thereby a paradox: through the townspeople's recognition of their mutual vulnerability, he becomes his own next victim—the lowest man in the kingdom, the condemned man—simultaneously with the highest (since the rank of Lord High Executioner is the highest next to that of the Lawgiver himself). Ko-Ko thus points towards both The Misfit's paradoxical Jesus "who thown everything off balance"[5] by becoming simultaneously the lowest and the highest, the all-powerful Being who allows himself to be put to death, and towards The Misfit himself, who is the condemned-man-turned-executioner of the grandmother and her family.

The Mikado, accepting the logic underlying the townspeople's strategem, extends it by adopting a moral stance which links Titipu structurally with Georgia. Pooh-Bah explains: "Our logical Mikado, seeing no moral difference between the dignified judge who condemns a criminal to die, and the industrious mechanic who carries out the sentence, has rolled the two offices into one, and every judge is now his own executioner." O'Connor follows the pattern by rolling the two offices into one, requiring The Misfit to act as both "judge" and "mechanic."

However, the *OED* distinguishes two principal meanings of the verb "judge": I. "To try or pronounce sentence; to condemn"; and 2. "To form an opinion about; to estimate; to appraise." The first meaning is the more relevant to *The Mikado,* but it is The Misfit's interest in the second that leads to his carrying out the first. "My daddy," he confides to the grandmother, "said I was a different breed of dog from my brothers and sisters. 'You know,' Daddy said, 'it's some that can live their whole life out without asking about it and it's others has to know why it is, and this boy is one of the latters. He's going to be into everything!'" The Misfit is moved to pass sentence on individual cases by his impulse to philosophize on the nature of the circumstances which produce the individual cases: Since Jesus "has thown everything off balance . . . then it's nothing for you to do but enjoy the few minutes you got left the best way you can—by killing somebody or burning down his house or doing some other meanness to him. No pleasure but meanness." The fruits of this considered judgement are the decision to kill the family. The execution of Bailey together with his wife and children he delegates to Hiram and Bobby Lee; the execution of the grandmother he reserves—for reasons of narrative strategy suggested by *The Mikado*—for himself.

That the unanticipated, though very logical, corollary of the Mikado's "object all sublime"—the ironic transformation of victim into judge and executioner—helps account for O'Connor's conception of The Misfit should now be clear, but, as a matter of fact, the character in whom the judge-executioner pattern occurs most startlingly is not The Misfit but the grandmother herself. It is her case which is dramatized in the story; it is she whom O'Connor makes act out—for the most part unwittingly—the pattern of crime-punishment-victim-judge-executioner before the reader's disbelieving eyes. Indeed, she exhibits the pattern with a good deal more subtlety and complexity than The Misfit himself does. But The Misfit, as his name suggests, is a special case, while the grandmother is the average person who, by means of the savage logic of paradox (both *The Mikado's* and O'Connor's), is turned into the opposite of what she intended to be. Let us trace the pattern first, then, as she exhibits it.

The grandmother is established, in the story's abrupt opening sentence ("The grandmother didn't want to go to Florida") in terms of her "wants"—characteristically negative—and of the destinations she either rejects or aims at. She immediately begins to manipulate to achieve her goal of getting to Tennessee rather than to Florida, pointing out to her son Bailey with an air of self-satisfaction that an escaped convict is headed towards Florida: "I wouldn't take my children in any direction with a criminal like that aloose in it. I couldn't answer to my conscience if I did." The course of action she embarks on develops according to a Titipu logic unperceived by herself or those accompanying her to lead to an end other than that which she envisages: by sending the family mistakenly down the abandoned road, she unwittingly leads her child and his children in precisely the direction in which the criminal is "aloose"; by starting up suddenly in the car when she realizes her mistake—that she had led them down the road to her not-yet-abandoned "want" to go to Tennessee—

she lets the concealed denizen of Titipu, the cat Pitty Sing, "aloose" among them to cause the accident; by voicing her recognition of The Misfit, she seals her fate, sending them all to their ultimate destination.[6]

Bizarre as it sounds, her "crime" is nothing more than to want to go to Tennessee rather than to Florida, and to engage in manipulation to get there; her punishment is that she has to "answer to [her] conscience" for leading her family to their deaths and to lose her own life. The disproportion is scarcely less absurd than that of being decapitated for flirting. The logic, therefore, by which the grandmother becomes victim and executioner is easy enough to trace; it is perhaps more difficult to see her as "judge." Nevertheless, it is the handling of the "judge" aspect that reveals most clearly O'Connor's reworking of the *Mikado* material into something extraordinarily original. Understanding it requires turning to another character from *The Mikado,* one who has bequeathed to the grandmother her most notable characteristic, her defining of herself by her gentility.

This is Pooh-Bah, the courtier who sets out the Mikado's logic in combining the offices of judge and executioner. Pooh-Bah relates that when Ko-Ko, the condemned man, was released from prison to be made Lord High Executioner, all the great officers of state resigned in a body because they were too proud to serve under a former criminal. Pooh-Bah thereupon allowed himself to be persuaded to accept all their various offices to become Lord High Everything Else, an act which required him to mortify his family pride since, as he disarmingly confesses, "I am, in point of fact, a particularly haughty and exclusive person, of pre-Adamite ancestral descent. . . . my family pride is something inconceivable. I can't help it. I was born sneering" (349).[7]

Pooh-Bah is invited, in the course of Act I, to take on one more office, Lord High Substitute, which means putting his head on the block in place of Ko-Ko for whom a substitute victim is required. Pooh-Bah predictably declines, but the reasons he gives are instructive for understanding O'Connor's conception of the grandmother. He advances family pride as the reason why he is simultaneously obliged both to accept and decline the honour: "I am so proud, / If I allowed / My family pride / To be my guide, / I'd volunteer / To quit this sphere / Instead of you, / In a minute or two" (364). Family pride must be "mortified," however; humility forbids him to make such a straightforwardly heroic gesture.

Family pride has two sides according to Pooh-Bah: the first is the *noblesse oblige* dimension which inspires man to rise magnanimously to heroic challenges; the second is the exploitative dimension which tempts man to use his gentility merely to avoid unpleasantness. Pooh-Bah achieves the second by paying lip-service to the first; in the very act of acknowledging that *noblesse* does oblige him to put himself forward as voluntary victim, he parodies the obligation by ironically turning it into self-promotional capital—advancing it as a reason why he should *not* have to die.

The grandmother's conception of gentility is altogether shabbier; that *noblesse* should oblige her to anything does not enter her head, although she is as quick as Pooh-Bah to lay the obligation on others. For her, gentility is a pure and simple defense against unpleasantness. "Does it seem right to you, lady,"[8] The Misfit asks the grandmother, "that one is punished a heap and another ain't punished at all?" The grandmother's response—the exchange takes place between the off-stage shootings of her daughter-in-law and of her two remaining grandchildren—is to use both The Misfit's gentility and her own as the reason why *she* should not have to die. "'Jesus!' the old lady cried. 'You've got good blood! I know you wouldn't shoot a lady! I know you come from nice people! Pray! Jesus, you ought not to shoot a lady'" (28). She advances *his* gentility as the reason he should not kill her; *hers* as the reason she should not have to die.[9]

O'Connor has been careful to establish this pattern back in the very first exchange between The Misfit and the grandmother, precisely at the point at which the old lady voiced her recognition of the stranger *as* The Misfit:

> "You wouldn't shoot a lady, would you?" the grandmother said and removed a clean handkerchief from her cuff and began to slap at her eyes with it.
>
> The Misfit pointed the toe of his shoe into the ground and made a little hole and then covered it up again. "I would hate to have to," he said.

The mordancy of The Misfit's answering gesture in this opening joust indicates how very mistaken the grandmother is in advancing her gentility as a defense against the threat he represents. Indeed, the futility of reliance on her shabbily self-interested conception of gentility has already been signalled by the flimsiness of the genteel paraphernalia with which she has equipped herself for the journey—the "clean handkerchief," accessory to the "navy blue straw sailor hat" and the "navy blue dress with a small white print," worn so that "in case of an accident, anyone seeing her dead on the highway would know at once that she was a lady"—and by the emptiness of her defensive slapping gesture.

Unfortunately for her, however, *noblesse* carries no more sense of obligation for him than it does for her:

> "Listen," the grandmother almost screamed, "I know you're a good man. You don't look a bit like you have common blood. I know you must come from nice people!"
>
> "Yes mam," he said, "finest people in the world."

The grandmother's threadbare genteel vocabulary—"lady," "good," "common," "nice," "fine"—stands in need of redefinition, which the tale proceeds to give it. Lacking any glimmer of the magnanimity or generosity inherent in true gentility, she is pushed by the pressure of events towards a perception of the terrifying demands of gentility in its root meaning, which the *OED* gives as from "L. *gentilis*, of the same *gens* or race." The moment at which the old lady makes the breakthrough to this level of understanding is, though she is scarcely aware of it, clearly marked for the reader as a moment of vision:

> The grandmother's head cleared for an instant. She saw the man's face twisted close to her own as if he were going to cry and she murmured, "Why, you're one of my babies. You're one of my own children!" She reached out and touched him on the shoulder. The Misfit sprang back as if a snake had bitten him and shot her three times through the chest.

The grandmother, at this moment when her "head clear[s]," becomes the "good man" who is so hard to find, precisely because she abandons her hold on gentility as a defense, a means of keeping the unpleasant "other" at a distance.[10] *Noblesse oblige:* she acknowledges her kinship with, her motherhood of, The Misfit. That the grandmother should be executed at the very moment she becomes "good"—indeed *because* she has become "good"—is the final link in the paradoxical chain of logic. Having been made the inadvertent executioner of her family, she transcends the threat posed by The Misfit by reaching a new, altruistic level of judgement about him, the consequence of which is death.[11] In her momentary clarity of vision, the grandmother judges The Misfit and herself to be members essentially of the same race—the human—and reaches out to seal the kinship with an embrace. The Misfit ratifies his name by his violent repudiation of the kinship. Yet the kinship *is* there, and a glance back at Pooh-Bah in *The Mikado* will help illuminate its nature. Pooh-Bah is haughtily exclusive because he considers himself to be of "pre-Adamite ancestral descent" (349). The grandmother, having set herself apart from "common" man, learns now that The Misfit is one of her "own," that they are both children of Adam. As Pooh-Bah would have died at the hands of Ko-Ko, the executioner whose place he would be taking had he followed the demands of gentility, so the grandmother dies at the hands of The Misfit in answer to his question, "Does it seem right to you, lady, that one is punished a heap and another ain't punished at all?" All the children of Adam are born to be punished by suffering and death; the grandmother's acknowledgement—however muddled—of this mystery of kinship earns her the right to the title, "lady."

But now it is time to return to the prototype, Pitty Sing, who suggested all these connections, and trace the geometrically precise role O'Connor has assigned to him. Although mentioned early in the story, he does not enter the action properly speaking until he is inadvertently released from his hiding place in the car and causes the accident. He then disappears again until just after the grandmother's death, when he returns to offer himself to The Misfit who, surprisingly, responds by picking him up.

The sequence, however, can be described from a quite different perspective: the grandmother (we may say) initiates the action by bringing Pitty Sing with her; Pitty Sing, accidentally made a free agent, initiates a specific sequence of events and disappears while The Misfit completes the sequence; Pitty Sing reappears, identifies with The Misfit, an identification which The Misfit accepts. The cat, therefore, begins by being identified with the grandmother; having helped bring about the grandmother's death, he then identifies with her murderer. Clearly, the relationship of both cat and convict to the grandmother is primarily structural; the clue to how it works lies with Pitti-Sing, the prototype.

The original Pitti-Sing is one of two companions of Yum-Yum, the heroine of *The Mikado*. The grouping of the girls as a threesome—they introduce themselves rather insistently in their opening trio as "Three little maids from school"—suggests a model for O'Connor's gangster trio as they step out of their "hearse-like" automobile and arrange themselves around their "scholarly" leader in front of the shaken family.

The primary note associated with the girls throughout the operetta is mockery. They begin, on their entry, by attacking the pretensions of Pooh-Bah (the incarnation of virtually every aspect of the status quo) to gentility, and his condescension towards their youth ("Go away, little girls. Can't talk to little girls like you. Go away" [358]), a condescension echoed by the grandmother ("In my time children were more respectful of their native states and their parents and everything else").

Ko-Ko, the Lord High Executioner, oscillating ambivalently between his roles as society's victim and its sanctioned exterminator, participates in the mockery of Pooh-Bah in a way which provides a pattern for The Misfit's ambiguous gallantry towards the grandmother. "Don't laugh at him, he can't help it," Ko-Ko explains in an aside to the girls; "Never mind them, they don't understand the delicacy of your position" (359), he reassures Pooh-Bah *sotto voce*. The Misfit apologizes for Bailey's outburst of profanity at his mother, "Lady, don't you get upset. Sometimes a man says things he don't mean. I don't reckon he meant to talk to you thataway," and then, as he sends Bailey off to be shot, he apologizes without a hint of a smile for not having a shirt on before the "ladies."[12]

Any member of the trio of school-girl mockers might perhaps have made a natural prototype for the cat who will permanently end the grandmother's pretensions to gentility, but what presumably caught O'Connor's attention about Pitti-

Sing is the fact that, of the three, she alone is witness to an execution.[13] The *Mikado* execution (Act II) is, to be sure, not real but fictional. It is fabricated by Ko-Ko, Pooh-Bah, and Pitti-Sing to appease the Mikado who, arriving unexpectedly, wants to hear the details of all recent executions. None having taken place, they invent one. The fictional *Mikado* execution provided O'Connor with a number of features which she incorporated into her handling of the grandmother's death. I would now like to trace those.

Ko-Ko, the prototype for The Misfit, sings the first stanza, setting out, in the *persona* of the executioner, the preparations for the decapitation: "The criminal cried, as he dropped him down, / In a state of wild alarm— / With a frightful, frantic, fearful frown, / I bared my big right arm. . . . Oh, never shall I / Forget the cry, / Or the shriek that shrieked he, / As I gnashed my teeth, / When from its sheath / I drew my snickersnee!" (385).

Two moments in this narration find an echo in "A Good Man." The first, the threatening menace of the executioner in the opening quatrain causing the criminal to "[drop] him down," reappears in the climax of The Misfit's apologia just before he kills the grandmother: "'Then it's nothing for you to do but enjoy the few minutes you got left the best way you can—by killing somebody or burning down his house or doing some other meanness. . . .' he said and his voice had become almost a snarl".

In the state of "wild alarm" produced by this theological onslaught, the grandmother squirms, struggles, and mumbling, "Maybe He didn't raise the dead," sinks down in the ditch.

The second, more emphatic, echo from Ko-Ko's narration ("Oh, never shall I / Forget the cry . . .") produces one of the most electrifying moments in the dialogue between the old lady and her killer. The second group of shots—those killing her daughter-in-law and her two remaining grandchildren—is heard from the woods:

> There were two more pistol reports and the grandmother raised her head like a parched old turkey hen crying for water and called, "Bailey Boy, Bailey Boy!" as if her heart would break.
>
> "Jesus was the only One that ever raised the dead," The Misfit continued.

The grandmother's crying-out signals a crucial change of direction for her on the road out of Titipu. She cries out to/for her son who is in fact already dead, killed by the first pair of shots. The poignancy of the moment comes in part from the homeliness of the parched turkey hen metaphor; its significance lies in her calling out not on behalf of herself but for another person. The breaking of her heart moves her towards the disinterested maternal love that becomes both her nemesis and her glory. The Misfit's sardonic response—"Jesus was the only One that ever raised the dead"—cannot halt her approaching readiness, almost in spite of herself, to offer The Misfit a place to "fit," the place of the Bailey Boy he has just murdered.

The second stanza of the execution narration, belonging to Pitti-Sing, I will return to in a moment. Pooh-Bah describes, in the final stanza, what happens immediately after the victim has been executed: "Now though you'd have thought that head was dead / (For its owner dead was he), / It stood on its neck, with a smile well-bred, / And bowed three times to me! / It was none of your impudent off-hand nods, / But as humble as could be; / For it clearly knew / The deference due / To a man of pedigree!" (380).

This underpins the grandmother's reliance on her own gentility as *the* quality which will see her through safely into the next world ("anyone seeing her dead on the highway would know at once that she was a lady"). The smile Pooh-Bah discerns on the corpse acknowledging his pedigree is echoed on the grandmother's dead face: "Hiram and Bobby Lee returned from the woods and stood over the ditch, looking down at the grandmother who half sat and half lay in a puddle of blood with her legs crossed under her like a child's and her face smiling up at the cloudless sky." The fact is, her gentility *has* seen her through; however, it is gentility now made authentic, as I suggested a moment ago, by its disinterested acknowledgement of kinship with The Misfit, acceptance of his pedigree as one of her "own children." Her smile is now directed towards that "cloudless sky" which is, in effect, the sky of *Wise Blood,* carrying on above the unseeing eyes of Hazel Motes and the inhabitants of Taulkinham its "vast construction work that involved the whole order of the universe and would take all time to complete."[14]

The stanza Gilbert assigns Pitti-Sing narrates the moment of execution: "He shivered and shook as he gave the sign / For the stroke he didn't deserve; / When all of a sudden his eye met mine, / And it seemed to brave his nerve . . . / As the sabre true / Cut cleanly through / His cervical vertebrae! / When a man's afraid, / A beautiful maid / Is a cheering sight to see; / And it's oh, I'm glad, / That moment sad / Was soothed by the sight of me!"

The primary point of connection between the two Pitti-Sings is that each is a witness to and implicated in an execution. The two moments made to stand out in Gilbert's version—when the victim's eye suddenly meets Pitti-Sing's and the moment "sad" when the victim is "soothed" by the sight of her—are particularly helpful in clarifying the intricacies of the role relationships among the grandmother, The Misfit, and the cat. Understanding Pitty Sing's role in the action from the beginning will clarify his role in the grandmother's execution.

Essentially, Pitty Sing functions as a double of the

grandmother (much the way Enoch Emery, Solace Layfield, and others act for Hazel Motes in *Wise Blood*), expressing a dimension of her self of which she is largely unaware. The nature of that aspect, pointed to by the *Mikado* prototype, becomes clear when we trace the operation of the double. The morning of the trip, the grandmother is "first one in the car, ready to go." The first mention of the cat follows immediately: "[The grandmother] had her big black valise that looked like the head of a hippopotamus in one corner, and underneath it she was hiding a basket with Pitty Sing, the cat, in it." The point of the oddly incongruous "head of a hippopotamus" image is twofold: "hippopotamus" obviously suggests the size, colour, and shape of the valise, but the relevance of the "head" emerges only—if at all—with the announcement of the cat's name and the reader's retroactive realization that the cat's prototype appears in a work dominated by the threat of decapitation. The cat is a concealed, forbidden presence in the car. The grandmother's reason for bringing the cat against her son's wishes—her fear that, left on his own, Pitty Sing might unwittingly bring about his own death—ironically figures forth the direction her own life is about to take because of her insistence of bringing Pitty Sing with her on the journey.

The grandmother's other reason for not wanting to leave Pitty Sing behind ("because he would miss her too much") suggests both the symbolic identification between the two and the grandmother's ignorance of Pitty Sing's true nature. The ground underlying both these reasons is her narcissistic wilfulness ("*She didn't intend* for the cat to be left alone") which opposes itself to Bailey's wishes ("*He didn't like* to arrive at a motel with a cat" [emphases added]). Pitty Sing functions essentially as an extension of the grandmother's wilfulness.

The journey begins; Pitty Sing remains quiescent while the grandmother takes "cat naps." The grandmother continues to pursue her own will by "craftily" manipulating the children ("Not telling the truth but wishing she were")[15] to "yell and scream" until their father agrees to take them to the house which represents the imperfectly remembered desires of her youth. Bailey unwittingly underlines the portentousness of the decision: "All right . . . but get this: this is the only time we're going to stop for anything like this. This is the one and only time." When the grandmother suddenly realizes as they drive down the abandoned road that she has led them in the wrong direction, her startled reaction frees Pitty Sing to act out her—the grandmother's—wilfulness without any hindrance. The result is the car crash, after which Pitty Sing disappears.

The passage in which Pitty Sing makes his startlingly graphic entry into the tale as an active agent repays close analysis:

> The road [to the grandmother's remembered plantation] looked as if no one had traveled on it in months.
>
> "It's not much farther," the grandmother said and just as she said it, a horrible thought came to her. The thought was so embarrassing that she turned red in the face and her eyes dilated and her feet jumped up, upsetting her valise in the corner. The instant the valise moved, the newspaper top she had over the basket under it rose with a snarl and Pitty Sing, the cat, sprang onto Bailey's shoulder.

The grandmother's "thought"—the sudden realization that she has been betrayed by the determined, narcissistic "wanting" which has dominated her since the story's opening sentence—triggers off a series of reactions in which the parts of her body and her suitcase take on an identity and life of their own (like the head of the hippopotamus or the head which "bowed three times" to Pooh-Bah) and act out, independently, the meaning and consequences of the perception she has just had: "Her eyes dilated . . . her feet jumped up. . . . the valise moved, the newspaper top . . . rose with a snarl," climaxing in "and Pitty Sing, the cat, sprang."

The cat's spring metamorphoses into another grotesque decapitation image: "Bailey remained in the driver's seat with the cat . . . clinging to his neck like a caterpillar." The causal connection between the grandmother's "thought" and the accident having been established ("The horrible thought she had before the accident was that the house she had remembered so vividly was not in Georgia but in Tennessee"), Bailey "removed the cat from his neck with both hands and flung it out the window against the side of a pine tree." While Bailey is still "in the driver's seat," he violently rejects the cat, real and symbolic, and steps out onto the road, unaware that he is in a landscape controlled by the logic of *The Mikado;* his own and his family's execution thereby become inevitable. Inevitable because, although Pitty Sing has vanished, the grandmother is about to meet and be driven by her impetuous wilfulness to recognize the agent destined to continue the process of destruction set in motion by Pitty Sing. Or, to put it in literary terms, The Misfit is about to take over Pitty Sing's role as double to the grandmother.

Many readers of "A Good Man" have been puzzled by the grandmother's initial reaction to The Misfit: "The grandmother had the peculiar feeling that the bespectacled man was someone she knew. His face was as familiar to her as if she had known him all her life but she could not recall who he was." Identifying him a few minutes later as The Misfit, she cries, "I recognized you at once!" What is clear to the reader is that she didn't recognize him as something (or someone) who has always been present in her life but as something or someone she cannot yet put a name to; she recognizes him as that aspect of herself which has been present since the first sentence, that aspect which has till now found its symbolic expression in Pitty Sing. Bailey having flung Pitty Sing temporarily out of the action, The Misfit takes over and extends Pitty Sing's function until Pitty Sing himself returns to endorse what has transpired in his absence.

The links between the cat and The Misfit are many, beginning with the cat's change of sex from female to male. The verbal associations are powerful. For example, The Misfit's first appearance is in the newspaper the grandmother is holding as the story opens, "rattling" it at Bailey, the same paper which makes its reappearance at the moment Pitty Sing is inadvertently turned loose by the grandmother. A quick reading of the passage might suggest that Pitty Sing springs up from *under* the "newspaper top" which conceals him—as in actuality he would—but the language embodies a more precise suggestion: "The instant the valise moved, the newspaper top she had over the basket under it rose with a snarl and Pitty Sing, the cat, sprang." That is to say, the decapitated head of the hippopotamus gets out of the way, the newspaper containing The Misfit rises with a snarl, and Pitty Sing springs to send the car into the ditch. The "snarl" emanating from the "newspaper top" recurs at that crucial moment of the story when The Misfit reaches the climax of his frighteningly logical deductions from the proposition that Jesus "thown everything off balance": "'No pleasure but meanness,' he said and his voice had become almost a snarl."[16]

The re-entry of Pitty Sing into the story as The Misfit orders his men to "Take [the grandmother] off and thow her where you thown the others" is no more accidental, structurally speaking, than any other aspect of his role; neither is his cosily domesticated overture to The Misfit, nor The Misfit's acceptance of the offered identification. The shocking juxtaposition of The Misfit's answering gesture to the cat—picking it up—with his brutality to the grandmother—shooting her three times "through the chest" merely because she touched him—is a typical O'Connor procedure in this story, but it should not divert us from seeing that, primarily, the function of this final gesture is to express the oneness of Pitty Sing with The Misfit.

The two aspects of the *Mikado* execution emphasized

by Gilbert's Pitti-Sing, the moment at which the victim's eye met hers and the sense that her presence "soothed that moment sad" for the victim, are both thematically relevant to and intertwined with "A Good Man Is Hard to Find." Since the grandmother reaches the same eye-level as The Misfit only when she sinks to the ground under his snarling "No pleasure but meanness," it is then that, her "head clear[ing]," she sees "the man's face twisted close to her own," and reaches out to him compassionately. As in *The Mikado,* the victim looks at the executioner: the expression on his face ("as if he were going to cry") precipitates the gesture which in its turn precipitates the shot. But if the grandmother's touch prompts The Misfit to kill her, it is what he has not been able to *see* that is at the root of his reaction: "'I wasn't there so I can't say [Jesus] didn't [raise the dead],' The Misfit said. 'I wisht I had of been there,' he said, hitting the ground with his fist. 'It ain't right I wasn't there because if I had of been there I would of known. . . . and I wouldn't be like I am now.'" Not knowing because he wasn't there to see, he shoots her.

That the limitations on his vision are implicit in the Pitti-Sing perspective is clear from the careful juxtaposition O'Connor makes between the two gestures she now gives The Misfit. He puts away his glasses as a prelude to picking up the cat:

> Then he put his gun down on the ground and took off his glasses and began to clean them. . . . Without his glasses, The Misfit's eyes were red-rimmed and pale and defenseless-looking. "Take her off and thow her where you thown the others," he said, picking up the cat that was rubbing itself against his leg.

The glasses, in conjunction with the return of Pitty Sing, help chart The Misfit's spiritual course in the last moments of the story. The "scholarly look" they endowed him with on his first appearance established his connection with the *Mikado* schoolgirl whose function is to mock; removing the glasses, he removes the mocking perspective, allowing him to look as "defenseless" as the old lady now lying in the ditch with "her legs crossed under her like a child's."[17] The last thing O'Connor would do, however, is sentimentalize this moment of vulnerability;[18] indeed, the removal of the glasses enables The Misfit to see and pronounce a very hard truth—a sardonic version of Pitti-Sing's "sooth[ing] that moment sad" for her victim and the only eulogy the grandmother will enjoy: "She would of been a good woman . . . if it had been somebody there to shoot her every minute of her life." Cold comfort, the reader may well feel; but O'Connor is merely being relentlessly—albeit characteristically—precise. The eulogy is "sooth[ing]" to the exact degree allowed by the compassionate ferocity, the paradoxical theological perspective, expressed in the excerpt from St. Cyril of Jerusalem which O'Connor chose as the epigraph to the collection in which "A Good Man" figures as the title-story: "The dragon is by the side of the road, watching those who pass. Beware lest he devour you. We go to the father of souls, but it is necessary to pass by the dragon."[19]

The ironically sentimental tableau made by Pitty Sing and The Misfit—the killer cuddling the pussy-cat—represents, in structural terms, the grandmother's apparent defeat at the hands of her "dragon." While the obvious dragon waiting by the side of the road may indeed have been The Misfit, it was Pitty Sing who, in an immediate sense, brought her to the rendezvous. However, what is even clearer is that both these dragons are, as symbolic extensions of the grandmother's own inadequacies, interiorized dragons. The grandmother's rendezvous on her way to "the father of souls" is, in the last analysis, with herself.

The tale's closing moment is a tableau in which Pitty Sing and The Misfit, joined by Bobby Lee, recreate the schoolgirls' opening trio, while refining the nature of the sardonicism their predecessors expressed. The girls sang:

YUM-YUM:	Everything is a source of fun! (*Chuckle*).
PEEP-BO:	Nobody's safe, for we care for none! (*Chuckle*).
PITTI-SING:	Life is a joke that's just begun! (*Chuckle*).

"Some fun!" is Bobby Lee's verdict, echoing Yum-Yum as he "slid[es] down the ditch" with a "yodel" instead of a "chuckle." The Misfit, for his part, has made it a clean sweep—"Nobody's safe"—by finishing off the family in the person of the grandmother. Nevertheless, with glasses off and Pitty Sing in his arms, The Misfit is moved to stretch his vision beyond the restrictions of his own earlier perspective ("No pleasure but meanness"). Bobby Lee's facile enjoyment is curtly dismissed ("Shut up, Bobby Lee"); Pitti-Sing's "Life is a joke!" has gone sour. Facing up to the implications of the epigraph, he utters a disclaimer that is also the bottom line: "It's no real pleasure in life."

Notes

1. The name is spelled Pitti-Sing in *The Mikado;* O'Connor changed it to Pitty Sing. She also changed the sex of the cat to male for reasons which will emerge. Presumably the name is in some way derived from a child's or elderly person's lisping version of "pretty thing." All quotations from *The Mikado* are taken from W. S. Gilbert and Sir Arthur Sullivan, *The Complete Plays of Gilbert and Sullivan* (New York: Modern Library, 1936).

2. The latest commentator, Alison R. Ensor, "Flannery O'Connor and Music," *Flannery O'Connor Bulletin* 14 (1985), 10, noting that to make the punishment fit the crime "is surely as much The Misfit's goal as it was the Mikado's," rejects the possibility of

substantial connection. Conjecture along these lines is, in her view, "possibly too elaborate. It hardly seems likely that someone so little acquainted with music as O'Connor would even know a very popular Gilbert and Sullivan operetta well enough to use it in such a way." This is to miss the point that the connection is literary, not musical.

While the biographical evidence indeed suggests that it is unlikely O'Connor knew the operetta in its full form, nevertheless it is commonplace knowledge that she was an enthusiastic reader of humor, especially the sardonic. Her letters and occasional prose testify that, despite her disclaimers of expertise in matters such as contemporary film and other writers, she had informed and decided tastes about comedy as a genre. The libretto to *The Mikado* was not difficult to come by even before the Modern Library edition of 1936 made it readily available.

3. *The World of Flannery O'Connor* (Bloomington: Indiana University Press, 1970), 20. A more recent evaluation of the cat's role by Stephen R. Portch, *The Explicator,* 37 (1978), 19–20, suggests that The Misfit's apparent acceptance of an alliance with the cat comes from a moment's softening, of "unconscious warmth," symbolized by The Misfit's removing his glasses. There is something to this, but it teeters on the edge of a sentimentality quite foreign to O'Connor. A third critic, the most astute to have yet written on O'Connor, Frederick Asals, in *Flannery O'Connor: The Imagination of Extremity* (Athens: University of Georgia Press, 1982), gives passing mention to the cat in the course of a brilliant analysis of the tale.

4. In one of her occasional pieces, "The Teaching of Literature," O'Connor writes that "the fiction writer is concerned with mystery that is lived. He's concerned with ultimate mystery as we find it embodied in the concrete world of sense experience." Cited here from *Mystery and Manners,* ed. Sally and Robert Fitzgerald (New York: Farrar, Straus and Giroux, 1969), 125.

5. In the original version of "A Good Man Is Hard to Find," O'Connor has The Misfit lapse into dialect at specific moments. Subsequent editions silently corrected "thown" to "thrown" until the Harvest reprint of the original edition appeared with the word restored to its original form.

6. O'Connor remarked in the introduction to a reading she gave of the story that "the old lady lacked comprehension, but . . . she had a good heart." *Mystery and Manners,* 110.

7. *The Mikado* contains another parodic gentility figure, Ka-

tisha, an elderly female of ludicrous pretentiousness, who allies herself with the convict executioner when she is rejected by the Mikado's son. She suggests a number of interesting connections with the grandmother which may be worth mentioning, though they cannot be pursued in the present context. She is self-willed; she both identifies with, and sets herself above, the Lawmaker and everyone else ("You wouldn't shoot a lady") basing her superiority and her immunity from the law of life and death on her "good blood"; she is deceived into losing faith in her intended ("Maybe He didn't raise the dead") and reaches out, as a consequence, to embrace the criminal-executioner.

8. The parodic form of genteel address is part of The Misfit's consistently respectful behaviour towards the grandmother.

9. Asals notes that the grandmother stands "looking down" on The Misfit throughout most of their dialogue. It will be clear that my analysis of the interaction between the grandmother and The Misfit, though done from a different perspective, is indebted to the parameters Asals outlines for the scene.

10. O'Connor commented, in the same introduction to the public reading I referred to earlier, on this moment: "The Grandmother is at last alone, facing the Misfit. Her head clears for an instant and she realizes, even in her limited way, that she is responsible for the man before her and joined to him by ties of kinship which have their roots deep in the mystery she has been merely prattling about so far." *Mystery and Manners*, 111–112.

11. O'Connor seems here to have drawn once again on T. S. Eliot whose poem *The Waste Land* so markedly influenced *Wise Blood*. Eliot writes in "The Dry Salvages": "You can receive this: / 'On whatever sphere of being / The mind of man may be intent / At the time of death'— / That is the one action / (And the time of death is every moment) / Which shall fructify in the lives of others" (lines 156–160).

12. The tale's symbolic design ensures that The Misfit, having buried his clothes (cf. Enoch Emery in Chapter 12 of *Wise Blood*), will have donned the dead Bailey's shirt by the time the grandmother recognizes him as one of her "own children."

13. Josephine Hendin's suggestion that O'Connor chose Pitti-Sing instead of her fellow-schoolgirls because Pitti-Sing "remarks in a sprightly way" to Yum-Yum, "Well, dear, it can't be denied that the fact your husband is to be beheaded in a month does seem to take the

top off it, you know" is not very helpful. Indeed, the fact that Gilbert gave the line to Peep-Bo rather than to Pitti-Sing makes it no help at all.

14. *Wise Blood* (New York: Farrar, Straus and Giroux, 1962), 37. Asals is helpful once again. He points out (53) the suggestion of "transcendent order" inherent in the *Wise Blood* passage but notes that while Hazel Motes's knees bend under him and he sits down, he "searches the sky for a sign as desperately and as futilely" as The Misfit later will. However, the grandmother *smiles* at the sky, which, since *Wise Blood,* has become—for her at least at this moment—cloudless.

15. The chorus's comment on Pooh-Bah (the grandmother's prototype) as he recounts his version of the execution is: "This haughty youth, / He speaks the truth / Whenever he finds it pays . . ." (387).

16. Asals notes the verbal connection between the cat's snarl and The Misfit's.

17. The device is similar but opposite to that used in connection with the "Bible-reading" glasses Hazel Motes inherits from his mother. Hazel needs to put the glasses on to get a truer perspective, e.g., to recognize the mummy as the new Jesus when Sabbath brings it to him in a Madonna tableau, whereas removing the "scholarly" glasses enables The Misfit to see more deeply. An interesting gloss on this latter phenomenon is O'Connor's remark in "The Teaching of Literature" that she felt that the then-current generation of students had been "made to feel that the aim of learning is to eliminate mystery." *Mystery and Manners,* 125.

18. O'Connor diagnoses the error of the teacher who told his students that "morally the Misfit was several cuts above the Grandmother" by declaring, "He had a really sentimental attachment to the Misfit." *Mystery and Manners,* 110.

19. O'Connor points to the centrality of the epigraph when, quoting it in "The Fiction Writer and His Country," she says, "No matter what form the dragon may take, it is of this mysterious passage past him, or into his jaws, that stories of any depth will always be concerned to tell." *Mystery and Manners,* 35.

MARY JANE SCHENCK

Deconstructed Meaning in ["A Good Man Is Hard to Find"]

Many contemporary theories of criticism address problems of meaning based on philosophies of language and the aesthetics of reception, so we worry less today about the author's conscious intentions than in previous times. Nevertheless, interpreting works of an author who has commented extensively on his or her own art may still be considered presumptuous. When the author has offered religious interpretations, counterarguments may seem to border on the heretical. Such are the risks for critics attempting to discuss how the fiction of Flannery O'Connor creates meanings in addition to or in contrast with what she herself said about her work.

O'Connor frequently commented on the Catholic faith, which she insisted formed her work, and most critics accept her own exegetical interpretations of her bizarre and troubling stories. Although the stories seem too brutal to be illustrations of Christian doctrine, at least as we conventionally conceive of it, O'Connor was able to justify her preoccupation with the ugly and grotesque by insisting on the writer's role as a prophet who must shake the reader and open his complacent eyes to reality and the need for grace. She was quite emphatic about the didactic function of the narrated events for both

---

Originally published as "Deconstructed Meaning in Two Short Stories by Flannery O'Connor" in *Ambiguities in Literature and Film,* ed. Hans P. Braendlin (Tallahassee: Florida State University Press, 1988), 125–135.

characters and readers, though the complications of interpreting her stories arise from the fact that they are not straightforward narratives like parables or exempla. Her texts are thoroughly ironic, and her use of irony creates ambiguities that undercut her own interpretations, even suggesting opposite ones, as other critics have suggested.[1]

What I would like to do is consider the ironic language of the texts in light of what Baudelaire in "De l'Essence du Rire" and Paul de Man in "The Rhetoric of Temporality" have revealed about this figure. For Baudelaire, comedy results from a doubling of spectator and laughable object or person. The heightened form of comedy, called irony, is in part an internalized doubling; it is a capacity to be at once self and other. As de Man explains:

> The *dedoublement* thus designates the activity of a consciousness by which a man differentiates himself from the non-human world. . . . The reflective disjunction not only occurs *by means of* language as a privileged category, but it transfers the self out of the empirical world into a world constituted out of, and in, language. . . . Language thus conceived divides the subject into an empirical self, immersed in the world, and a self that becomes like a sign in its attempt at differentiation and self-definition.[2]

What de Man says of the ironic consciousness accurately depicts the method by which characters are created and create themselves in O'Connor's fiction. In "A Good Man Is Hard to Find" and "The River," characters consciously or unconsciously use both written and oral language as well as pictorial "texts" to create a doubled self to escape an empirical one. To the extent that they succeed, they illustrate the performative quality of language, momentarily creating reality rather than reflecting it. But most of O'Connor's characters fail to understand the performative and arbitrary nature of their language. The disastrous climaxes so characteristic of her fiction are created in part by the conflict between the two selves as well as the conflict between characters who all may be doubled. The ironic doubling leads to a complete disintegration of the self at the moment when the character must confront the absence of grounding behind the linguistic self. As de Man explains, this process is not a finite or affirmative one. It is a radical process of deconstruction leading to madness. In a statement that well could have been written about the ironic process in O'Connor's fiction, de Man says:

> Irony is unrelieved *vertige*, dizziness to the point of madness. Sanity can exist only because we are willing to function within the conventions of duplicity and dissimulation, just as social language dissimulates the inherent violence of relationships among human beings. Once this mask is shown to be a mask, the authentic being underneath appears necessarily as on the verge of madness.[3]

As we will see in the following discussion, the unmasking of language in O'Connor's stories leads very precisely to violence, if not madness.

"A Good Man Is Hard to Find" presents a masterful portrait of a woman who creates a self and a world through language. From the outset, the grandmother relies on "texts" to structure her reality. The newspaper article about The Misfit mentioned in the opening paragraph of the story is a written text which has a particular status in the narrative. It refers to events outside and prior to the primary *récit*, but it stands as an unrecognized prophecy of the events which occur at the end. For Bailey, the newspaper story is not important or meaningful, and for the grandmother it does not represent a real threat but is part of a ploy to get her own way. It is thus the first one of her "fictions," one which ironically comes true. The grandmother's whole personality is built upon the fictions she tells herself and her family. Although she knows Bailey would object if she brought her cat on the trip, the grandmother sneaks the cat into the car, justifying her behavior by imagining "he would miss her too much and she was afraid he might brush himself against one of the gas burners and accidentally asphyxiate himself." She also carefully cultivates a fiction about the past when people were good and when "children were more respectful of their native states and their parents and everything else." As she tells Red Sam at the Tower when they stop to eat, "People are certainly not nice like they used to be."

The grandmother reads fictional stories to the children, tells them ostensibly true stories, and provides a continual gloss on the physical world they are passing. "Little niggers in the country don't have things like we do. If I could paint, I'd paint that picture." Lacking that skill, the grandmother nevertheless verbally "creates" a whole universe as they ride along. "'Look at the graveyard!' the grandmother said, pointing it out. 'That was the old family burying ground. That belonged to the plantation.'" She creates the stories behind the visual phenomena she sees and explains relationships between events or her own actions which have no logic other than that which she lends them.

Her most important fiction is, of course, the story of the old plantation house which becomes more of an imperative as she tells it. The more she talks about it, the more she wants to see it again, so she does not hesitate to self-consciously lie about it. "'There was a secret panel in this house,' she said craftily, not telling the truth but wishing she were." At this point we see clearly the performative quality of the grandmother's language. At first it motivates her own desire, then spills over onto the children, finally culminating in their violent outburst of screaming and kicking to get their father to stop the car. The performative quality of her language becomes even more crucial when she realizes that she has fantasized the location of the house. She does not admit it, but her thoughts manifest themselves physically: "The thought was so embarrassing that she turned red in the face and her eyes dilated and her feet jumped up, upsetting her valise in the corner." Of course, it is her physical action which frees the cat and causes the accident. After the accident, she again fictionalizes about her condition, hoping she is injured so she can deflect Bailey's anger, and she cannot even manage to tell the truth about the details of the accident.

The scene with The Misfit is the apogee of the grandmother's use of "fictions" to explain and control reality, attempts that are thwarted by her encounter with a character who understands there is no reality behind her words. When the grandmother recognizes The Misfit, he tells her it would have been better if she hadn't, but she has *named* him, thus forcing him to become what is behind his self-selected name. In a desperate attempt to cope with the threat posed by the murderer, the grandmother runs through her litany of convenient fictions. She believes that there are class distinctions ("I know you're a good man. You don't look a bit like you have common blood"), that appearance reflects reality ("You shouldn't call yourself The Misfit because I know you're a good man at heart. I can just look at you and tell"), that redemption can be achieved through work ("You could be honest too if you'd only try. . . . Think how wonderful it would be to settle down . . ."), and finally, that prayer will change him ("'Pray, pray,' she commanded him").

In contrast to the grandmother, whose flood of questions, explanations, and exhortations accompany the sequence of murderous events, the mother and Bailey react only physically. Deprived of language, they are barely more than props in the drama unfolding around them. Even the grandmother soon starts to lose her voice, the only mechanism that stands between her and reality. When she does try to tell The Misfit he must pray, her language has become fractured; all that comes out is the end of a sentence. "She wanted to tell him that he must pray. She opened and closed her mouth several times before anything came out. Finally she found herself saying, 'Jesus, Jesus,' meaning, Jesus will help you, but the way she was saying it, it sounded as if she might be cursing." She finally loses control of her language and the myths they provide: "'Maybe He didn't raise the dead,' the old lady mumbled, not knowing what she was saying and feeling so dizzy that she sank down in the ditch with her legs twisted under her."

When she reaches out to touch The Misfit and says, "Why you're one of my babies. You're one of my own children," she either has uttered her final fantasy, having lost touch with reality as she confuses The Misfit (who is now wearing Bailey's shirt) with her own child, or she is attempting a last ingratiating appeal for his sympathies. O'Connor's interpretation of this line is that at this moment the grandmother realizes, "even in her limited way, that she is responsible for the man before her and joined to him by ties of kinship which have their roots deep in the mystery she has been merely prattling about so far."[4] This is one possible reading of the scene and in some quarters the accepted one, but we could also say that the grandmother simply is wrong again, and her comment provokes The Misfit into shooting her. Surely we witness here the moment when a clash of language creates the vertiginous movement of irony into violence and madness. The Misfit rejects her interpretations of his being and refuses to provide a grounding for that language. Her fictions are proven to be "just talk" and both her empirical and linguistic self are destroyed.

In counterpoint to the grandmother's slow destruction as each verbal system she has created fails to reflect the reality around her, The Misfit uses language literally to relate events, at the same time recognizing the dangerous power of words. His language accurately describes the accident scene: "'We turned over twice!' said the grandmother. 'Oncet,' he corrected. 'We seen it happen.'" He is the only one who seems to know that sometimes language fails utterly: "He seemed to be embarrassed as he couldn't think of anything to say."

His understanding of himself is grounded not in a knowledge of the events of his empirical self but in the recognition that language has created him. His father provided him an essence by describing him as "a different breed of dog." He knows that he has been or done various things in his life, but he is curiously unclear about the crime which sent him to jail. Nevertheless, he says his punishment is no mistake for two reasons—a written document says he committed it and a psychiatrist told him so. Even though he maintains it was a lie, he accepts the power of words to define his existence, and he knows that he should get things in writing in order to control his life. Since he cannot make sense of the events of his empirical self, he quite consciously creates a double by renaming himself The Misfit and living out its violent implications. The phenomenon of a character acquiring a new identity by using a new name is . . . the most explicit indication of the linguistically doubled self so crucial to the irony of th[is] text.

We might believe that The Misfit through his ironic vision has at least created a self that copes with the empirical world when he says, "It's nothing for you to do but enjoy the few minutes you got left the best way you can—by killing somebody or burning down his house or doing some other meanness to him. No pleasure but meanness." But in the very last line of the story, he deconstructs even this doubled self: "'Shut up, Bobby Lee,' The Misfit said. 'It's no real pleasure in life.'" His strange alternations between polite talk and cold-blooded murder and his last statement demonstrate the radical shifting back and forth between selves that cancel each other figuratively as he has literally cancelled the shifting consciousness of the grandmother. . . .

The difficulty in "reconstructing meaning," to use Wayne Booth's term, is that the central characters with whom we should identify or from whom we hope to grasp some sense of meaning dissolve before our eyes into non-beings. The frightening moment occurs when we witness the fictional self confront a challenge to the reality of that self. As de Man and Baudelaire have pointed out:

> The movement of the ironic consciousness is anything but reassuring. The moment the innocence or authenticity of our sense of being in the world is put into question, a far from harmless process gets underway. It may start as a casual bit of play with a stray loose end of the fabric, but before long the entire texture of the self is unraveled and comes apart.[5]

The personalities of these characters are created by language, and this language fails them in one of two circumstances. They either are confronted by the natural world whose laws mock their interpretations, or they are confronted by a character who understands that language is mere convention. If the conventions are not shared, the encounter will lead to devastating physical or emotional violence. Seen from this perspective, the events which may seem absurd at first now appear to be well motivated by language. All types of language—names, Bible stories, daydreams, myths, sermons, and newspaper articles—function to create characters and events. The people are separated from each other and their world through this language, but at the outset the alienation is merely a tension inhibiting communication. By the end, when the language of the doubled selves has been unmasked, the characters behind it are totally deconstructed and no longer exist. Kierkegaard refers to "the infinite elasticity of irony, the secret trap door through which one is suddenly hurled downward, not like the schoolmaster in *The Elfs* who falls a thousand fathoms, but into the infinite nothingness of irony."[6] In spite of her intentions to the contrary, at the end of O'Connor's stories we feel a sudden shock of recognition as we witness the unraveling of the characters' personalities. Like the characters' fictional selves, our own experience with the text is deconstructed as we sense ourselves "fall through the trap door," uncertain of where, or if, we will land on any firm ground of meaning.

Notes

1. Josephine Hendin, *The World of Flannery O'Connor* (Bloomington: Indiana University Press, 1970); Gilbert Muller, *Nightmares and Visions: Flannery O'Connor and the Catholic Grotesque* (Athens: University of Georgia Press, 1972); Dorothy Walters, *Flannery O'Connor* (New York: Twayne Publishers, Inc., 1973).

2. Paul de Man, "The Rhetoric of Temporality," *Interpretation: Theory and Practice,* ed. C. S. Singleton (Baltimore: Johns Hopkins Press, 1969), 195–196.

3. de Man, "Rhetoric," 198.

4. Dorothy T. McFarland, *Flannery O'Connor, Modern Literature Monographs* (New York: Ungar, 1976), 21–22.

5. de Man, "Rhetoric," 197.

6. Søren Kierkegaard, *The Concept of Irony,* trans. Lee Cappel (Bloomington: University of Indiana Press, 1965), 63.

Selected Bibliography

Works by Flannery O'Connor

FICTION

Wise Blood. New York: Harcourt, Brace and Company, 1952.

A Good Man Is Hard to Find and Other Stories. New York: Harcourt, Brace and Company, 1955.

The Violent Bear It Away. New York: Farrar, Straus and Cudahy, 1960.

Everything That Rises Must Converge. New York: Farrar, Straus and Giroux, 1965.

The Complete Stories. New York: Farrar, Straus and Giroux, 1971.

Flannery O'Connor: Collected Works. Edited by Sally Fitzgerald. New York: The Library of America, 1988.

NONFICTION

Mystery and Manners. Edited by Sally and Robert Fitzgerald. New York: Farrar, Straus and Giroux, 1969.

The Habit of Being: Letters of Flannery O'Connor. Edited by Sally Fitzgerald. New York: Farrar, Straus and Giroux, 1979.

Conversations with Flannery O'Connor. Edited by Rosemary M. Magee. Jackson: University Press of Mississippi, 1987.

Suggested Further Reading

BOOKS

Asals, Frederick. *Flannery O'Connor: The Imagination of Extremity.* Athens: University of Georgia Press, 1982.

Brinkmeyer, Robert H., Jr. *The Art and Vision of Flannery O'Connor.* Baton Rouge and London: Louisiana State University Press, 1989.

Browning, Preston M., Jr. *Flannery O'Connor.* Carbondale and Edwardsville: Southern Illinois University Press, 1974.

Driskell, Leon V. and Brittain, Joan T. *The Eternal Crossroads: The Art of Flannery O'Connor.* Lexington: University of Kentucky Press, 1971.

Eggenschwiler, David. *The Christian Humanism of Flannery O'Connor.* Detroit: Wayne State University Press, 1972.

Feeley, Kathleen. *Flannery O'Connor: Voice of the Peacock.* New Brunswick: Rutgers University Press, 1972.

Gentry, Marshall Bruce. *Flannery O'Connor's Religion of the Grotesque.* Jackson: University Press of Mississippi, 1986.

Giannone, Richard. *Flannery O'Connor and the Mystery of Love*. Urbana and Chicago: University of Illinois Press, 1989.

Hendin, Josephine. *The World of Flannery O'Connor*. Bloomington: Indiana University Press, 1970.

Kessler, Edward. *Flannery O'Connor and the Language of Apocalypse*. Princeton: Princeton University Press, 1986.

Martin, Carter W. *The True Country: Themes in the Fiction of Flannery O'Connor*. Nashville: Vanderbilt University Press, 1969.

May, John R. *The Pruning Word: The Parables of Flannery O'Connor*. Notre Dame: University of Notre Dame Press, 1976.

McFarland, Dorothy Tuck. *Flannery O'Connor*. New York: Frederick Ungar, 1976.

Montgomery, Marion. *Why Flannery O'Connor Stayed Home*. LaSalle, Illinois: Sherwood Sugden, 1981.

Muller, Gilbert H. *Nightmares and Visions: Flannery O'Connor and the Catholic Grotesque*. Athens: University of Georgia Press, 1972.

Orvell, Miles. *Invisible Parade: The Fiction of Flannery O'Connor*. Philadelphia: Temple University Press, 1972.

Paulson, Suzanne Morrow. *Flannery O'Connor: A Study of the Short Fiction*. Boston: Twayne Publishers, 1988.

Reiter, Robert. ed. *Flannery O'Connor*. St. Louis: B. Herder, 1968.

Stephens, Martha. *The Question of Flannery O'Connor*. Baton Rouge: Louisiana State University Press, 1973.

Walters, Dorothy. *Flannery O'Connor*. New York: Twayne Publishers, 1973.

ARTICLES

Cheney, Brainard. "Miss O'Connor Creates Unusual Humor Out of Ordinary Sin." *Sewanee Review* 71 (1963): 644–652.

Ellis, James. "Watermelons and Coca-Cola in 'A Good Man Is Hard to Find': Holy Communion in the South." *Notes on Contemporary Literature* 8 (1978): 7–8.

Kropf, C. R. "Theme and Setting in 'A Good Man Is Hard to Find'" *Renascence* 24 (1972): 177–180, 206.

Lasseter, Victor. "The Children's Names in Flannery O'Connor's 'A Good Man Is Hard to Find.'" *Notes on Modern American Literature* 6 (1982): item 6.

Lasseter, Victor. "The Genesis of Flannery O'Connor's 'A Good Man Is Hard to Find." *Studies in American Fiction* 10 (1982): 227–232.

Montgomery, Marion. "Miss Flannery's 'A Good Man,'" *Denver Quarterly* 3 (Autumn 1968): 1–19.

Portch, Stephen R. "O'Connor's 'A Good Man Is Hard to Find.'" *Explicator* 37 (Fall 1978): 19–20.

Quinn, John J., S.J. "A Reading of Flannery O'Connor [*i.e.*, 'A Good Man Is Hard to Find'']," *Thought* 48 (1973): 520–531.

Renner, Stanley. "Secular Meaning in 'A Good Man Is Hard to Find.'" *College Literature* 9 (1982): 123–132.

Richard, Claude. "Désir et Destin dans 'A Good Man Is Hard to Find.'" *Delta* 2 (1976): 61–74.

Sweet-Hurd, Evelyn. "Finding O'Connor's Good Man." *Notes on Contemporary Literature* 14 (1984): 9–10.

Thompson, Terry. "Doodlebug, Doodlebug: The Misfit in 'A Good Man Is Hard to Find,'" *Notes on Contemporary Literature* 17 (1987): 8–9.

———. "The Killers in O'Connor's 'A Good Man Is Hard to Find.'" *Notes on Contemporary Literature* 16 (1986): 4.

Walls, Doyle W. "O'Connor's 'A Good Man Is Hard to Find,'" *Explicator* 46 (Winter 1988): 43–45.

Woodward, Robert H. "A Good Route Is Hard to Find: Place Names and Setting in O'Connor's 'A Good Man Is Hard to Find.'" *Notes on Contemporary Literature* 3 (1973): 2–6.

Wray, Virginia. "Narration in *A Good Man Is Hard to Find*." *Publications of the Arkansas Philological Association* 14 (1988): 25–38.

Permissions

"A Good Man Is Hard to Find" from *A Good Man Is Hard to Find and Other Stories* by Flannery O'Connor. Copyright 1953 by Flannery O'Connor; renewed 1981 by Regina O'Connor, reprinted by permission of Harcourt Brace Jovanovich, Inc.

Excerpt from "On Her Own Work" from *Mystery and Manners* by Flannery O'Connor. Copyright 1969 by the Estate of Mary Flannery O'Connor; reprinted by permission of Farrar, Straus and Giroux, Inc.

"To John Hawkes" and "To a Professor of English" from *The Habit of Being: Letters of Flannery O'Connor.* Copyright 1979 by Regina O'Connor; reprinted by permission of Farrar, Straus and Giroux, Inc.

"A Good Source Is Not So Hard to Find" by J. O. Tate, from *The Flannery O'Connor Bulletin* 9 (1980): 98–103. Reprinted by permission.

"Reading the Map in 'A Good Man Is Hard to Find'" by Hallman B. Bryant, from *Studies in Short Fiction* 18 (1981): 301–307. Reprinted by permission of *Studies in Short Fiction,* Newberry College, South Carolina.

"Advertisements for Grace: Flannery O'Connor's 'A Good Man Is Hard to Find'" by W. S. Marks, III, from *Studies in Short Fiction* 4 (1966): 19–27. Reprinted by permission of *Studies in Short Fiction,* Newberry College, South Carolina.

"A Dissenting Opinion of Flannery O'Connor's 'A Good Man Is Hard to Find'" by William S. Doxey, from *Studies in Short Fiction* 10 (1973): 199–204. Reprinted by permission of *Studies in Short Fiction,* Newberry College, South Carolina.

"Everything Off Balance: Protestant Election in Flannery O'Connor's 'A Good Man Is Hard to Find'" by Michael O. Bellamy, from *The Flannery O'Connor Bulletin* 8 (1979): 116–124. Reprinted by permission.

"Flannery O'Connor's 'A Good Man Is Hard to Find' and G. K. Chesterton's *Manalive*" by William J. Scheick, from *Studies in American Fiction* 11 (1983): 241–245. Reprinted by permission.

"A Good Man's Predicament" by Madison Jones, from *The Southern Review* 20 (1984): 836–841. Reprinted by permission of the author.

"'The Meanest of Them Sparkled': Beauty and Landscape in Flannery O'Connor's Fiction" by Carter Martin, from *Realist of Distances: Flannery O'Connor Revisited,* 1987, reprinted courtesy of Aarhus University Press, Aarhus, Denmark.

"Cats, Crime, and Punishment: *The Mikado*'s Pitti-Sing in 'A Good Man Is Hard to Find'" by J. Peter Dyson, from *English Studies in Canada* 14 (1988): 436–452. Reprinted by permission.

"Deconstructed Meaning in ['A Good Man Is Hard to Find']" by Mary Jane Schenck, originally published as "Deconstructed Meaning in Two Short Stories by Flannery O'Connor" in *Ambiguities in Literature and Film,* ed. Hans P. Braendlin (Tallahassee: Florida State University Press, 1988), 125–135. Reprinted by permission.